I0673051

Two in a Lifetime

A Novel

Samuel Hudson

ISBN 978-0-578-34403-4

For A and our children.

Chapter 1

The lobster traps were stacked oddly as he walked up the beach towards the jetty, as if both had washed up to be noticed that way yellow and rusty. He looked out to the tide to see a single fishing boat bobbing close to the jetty bell. The sun was hot and the cloud cover was low as the day approached noon. He walked barefoot paying attention to the sea side cottages and beautiful homes along the beach front. He longed to be in a position one day to have such luck to own one of them, especially one with a tall flagpole to represent. The tide rolled over his feet cold. He could not get her off his mind and why he let her go, she was due to communicate. "What did she expect me to do? Why did she have to leave like that?" he said a loud, his body language was taken in by a couple as they walked by. *Was she looking for me to completely object, she knows the risk involved* he thought. Colin Sanderson suddenly made an appearance on the beach.

"Dude I knew I would find you out here at some point, where the hell have you been the last few days?" Colin asked.

"You know man," Jonas said briefly he wanted to keep walking.

"No. You don't reply, you don't respond, you need friends."

"I'm maintaining on my own, thank you," he said.

"Jo you missed one hell of a party last night; my place was full of women." Colin enthused.

Jonas stopped Colin in mid-step and became vibrant with his body language.

"So you think I should just move on! Just because Jess left doesn't mean we're over."

"Hey man I hate to break this to you, but she was leavin' regardless." Colin instantly regretted saying that he briefly closed his eyes, stepped back then dialed into his friend.

"Really, thanks asshole." Jonas immediately reacted.

"Dude, she has been talking about doing this mission work again for last three or so years now. She brings it up at every family function 'Children of West Indies' and so on. We could tell that she wasn't kidding around last week, you were either going with her or not, end of story." Colin thought he knew everything.

5

"You don't know shit, ok and lets leave it at that," he said.

He hated that about his friend. At times what he didn't know could fill a book. Colin is good people. Trustworthy.

"Whoa dude, you forget Jess is my cousin she has always been head strong especially her passion for children and charity."

Jonas looked off with the tide, then face to face with Colin.

"Hey man, I'm sorry. Not trying to be rude or insensitive here." Colin backed away.

"Are we ok?" Colin put his hand out towards Jonas then suddenly dropped his arm to his side. Jonas closed his eyes and pressed his fingers against the arch of his noise as if mentally exhausted.

"Yeah man, it's been a lot the last few days. You have no clue how dangerous it is down there, for real." His tone did not waiver.

Colin quickly changed the subject.

"Whataya doing later man?" Colin asked.

"No plans, as of now" he said as he shrugged his shoulders.

"We have more people coming over tonight, say uh-uh-uh, nine thirty or so." Colin turned around to the opposite direction and began to walk away, "And do me a favor.".... Colin turned back and pointed to Jonas.

"Yeah what's that?" Jonas asked.

"Don't fall trap to the blogosphere, face to face friends are what you need right now."

Jonas nodded and continued on thru the jetty parking lot towards the cottage. As Colin walked away the sun had abruptly disappeared behind the abrupt fog, like a sheen of bright dense smoke. Colin is one of the Sanderson bunch. Jonas was noticed walking from the view of their beach front mansion. The Sanderson family owns many beachfront and island properties. A very high profile family in the state, local Lions if ya know what I mean. The Sanderson family had done well in the insurance business and real estate dating back to WW II. At this point donating money was the real family business. Whichever charity or project that needed matching funds the Sanderson family was involved. There are six beaches in town the Sanderson family drives the bus on environmental beach cleanup after the tourists leave. The local folks say 'There ain't a check they can't write', at least that was the impression. They were silent donors to various churches and to the local hospital where Jonas worked.

Prior to Jessica leaving for the aide mission, her and Jonas were renting a cottage from late spring thru the summer. Jessica's aunt always gave her and Jonas a good deal on the seasonal rent. Jessica's family enjoyed their company for the summers. He remembered that she was drawn to this particular cottage with the lightness of the cedar shingles and the American flag mailbox. Jonas reached in the mailbox it couldn't have been fuller. He pulled a small box out and he gave it a look over. 'She left without her oils', he said to himself. Going thru the mail were bills upon bills mostly student loan debt and notification of events from their alma mater. The place where they met five years prior. They were in the early thirties now. He reminisced on how beautiful she was in the university library that day. She had very matter of fact presence about her, she did not mince words. Ever. Especially when she caught him starring at her in the library that day.

"Why don't you take a picture it will last longer?" she said sitting two tables away.

He was caught starring at her. She didn't even looked up from her book.

"I'm sorry I didn't mean to disturb you." He looked away in embarrassment.

She had gathered her books and slowly walked over to his side of the table.

Don't screw this up, he was nervous. All he could do was smile.

"Well it's too late now," she said. "You can buy me a pumpkin spice latte to make it up to me."

She returned the smile and winked at him. He remembered his quickness at which he gathered his belongings as he followed her out thru the hall and down the stairwell.

"I can't believe you actually spoke to me." he said.

"What?" She lightly laughed.

"That's an odd thing to say, isn't it?" Looking back at him.

"Not when you shy like me."

They laughed together he was beginning to feel on cloud nine.

"Oh wow look at them." she said.

They both took notice to the campus frisbee tournament in courtyard as they crossed over the sidewalk to the cafe house. The amount of participants rivaled an amphitheater concert. It was a beautiful sunny New England day full of fun and laughter on campus. He remembered he brought her latte as they sat and how oddly quiet it was that afternoon in the cafe.

"I'm Jonas Parker by the way." He smiled as he reached out his hand.

"Jessica Adams." The music in the café was light and had a calming effect.

"To be honest I was staring at you in two parts," he said.

"Really," she looked at him with curiosity.

"I think we have lab together," he said "Fisk?"

"Yes. I am not a fan of his."

"Me neither, I could take him or leave him." he said.

"Well we probably have different reasons, he wasn't very nice to a girlfriend of mine."

"Really, does she work for him or something?"

"She did, and she did not appreciate his flirty passes and told him so directly."

"No way, how did he take that?"

"Not well, it was drama and they've moved on, she started seeing Josh Michaels." She said then sipped her latte.

"Do you know him?" Jessica asked.

Jonas perked up.

"Name sounds familiar."

Jonas had no intention of mentioning that he had taken out an ex-girlfriend of Josh Michaels.

He took Jessica all in. Her light brown hair, blue eyes and her brown framed glasses.

"So you mentioned me in two parts, what was the other?" She inquired.

Jonas blinked with direct eye contact, "I think the other part is quite obvious." They both smiled at one another, Jessica leaned back in her chair.

"Jonas where are you from?" She asked. "I can tell you not from New England."

"How can you tell?" He replied. "You don't have an accent, or even a fake accent." She smiled to him.

"I'm originally from Rockport, Iowa." He looked to her with a raised brow.

"You're a long way from home," she said. "Iowa isn't home anymore."

He gathered himself in front of the mailbox and then walked to the back of the cottage to the back deck and opened the sliding door to the back sitting room. He flipped envelope by envelope he became a gasp by a letter addressed to him. It was from Jessica. The letter was post marked four days ago in Miami, when emotions were high.

Jo.

I'm writing this letter to you to avoid another shout matched phone call. I know you are upset with me given the short notice to this. My life's work comes in parts and phases. Two years ago we briefly went our separate ways. At that time it was unknown if we would come together again. I must confess that at times I feel getting back together was a mistake. But then other times I am grateful to God to have you in my life. I can't make sense of my feelings. Our peaks and valleys come in waves and I bare the same responsibility. I know and feel you love daily. However our priorities are not bonded. I am in an unsure place right now in heart, body, mind and soul. I will be with the aide group sailing for the Indies. There are many in need of medical attention on this mission. I'm sorry. With love. –Jess

Chapter 2

He grabbed his fishing pole and headed for the jetty, he had the good sense to clear his head. It wasn't a far walk but it would do. In a left handed way she is throwing the Indies in my face, he thought to himself. I went through more shit than anyone else. More than my fair share of hell. He had become diagnosed with a touch of malaria three years ago. He liked to tell people randomly that malaria would put King Kong on his ass.

Some years back the couple had volunteered as medical aide-workers in portions of the West Indies and various islands. Jonas reflected on what a tough six months that had been. Getting pushed to the brink of work in third world impoverished countries was one thing, being kidnapped for ransom was a whole other.

He remembered the terror the cartel put him under. There was not a day that he did not remember his kidnapping. After surviving that ordeal Jonas considered all other life experiences to be relative to those two days. He could never forget the kidnapper's voice:

"Hey Gringo you awake?" An intense Latin accent spoke out.

Jonas began to come back to consciousness, he knew he was not out long. He could still hear the noise of the nearby port crane, he remembered looking at it across the caisson before getting hit. He was now tied to a chair with a dark hood over his head. He felt what seemed like warm water being poured over him. He was bleeding, he felt concussed. He sighed in pain. "Yes, I am for now."

"You put up a fight back there in the street. I should kill you for busting my fucking jaw man. It took three of us to take you down, you damn lucky Raul wasn't with us. Raul woulda killed your gringo ass. Raul the badest mutha fucker in da Porto."

"You speak English huh, why don't you take this blind fold off, I'm bleeding from my head." Jonas replied.

Suddenly the cloth and tape was ripped off his head. The sting from the tape and the brightness of the room took him by surprise.

An intimidating dark skinned man glared at him and backhanded Jonas immediately. Jonas cringed and winced in pain. The man grabbed Jonas by his face, then abruptly moved behind him. Jonas saw his reflection in the mirror across the room beaten and bloody. He quickly glanced the room all the walls were a continuous mirror. There were five other men in the room all of them were armed. Two men with machetes the others had rifles similar to the ships security force. The dark skinned man was tall, his head was shaved and he wore dark sunglasses. He was clearly the alpha of this group.

"Gringo you speak when spoken to and no more, or will blow your fucking brains out, you see this gun I will use it."

He was speaking to Jonas from his reflection in the mirror pressing his pistol to back of his head.

Jonas closed his eyes, he felt the vibration of the hammer being cocked. Click, Snap. The man pulled the trigger. Jonas shook his head forward suddenly in total fear. He took a deep breath and let out a fearful sigh. All the men began laughing.

Jonas realized he was in a brothel or one of local whore houses. But he knew he was close to the ship with the sound of the cranes rolling track safety alarm sounding in the distance.

Just then the door opened and more locals came into the room. Some were local business girls he remembered seeing out in about in the city, sometimes at all hours. One girl was wearing medical scrubs donning a medical surgical mask and face shield. She walked into the bathroom with other men and the dark skinned man. He could hear them chatting a mixed Spanish or Portuguese. Jonas knew how to order drinks in both languages. Cuba libre translated in both languages for rum and diet soda. Gin and tonic he knew how to point out from the bar.

The dark skinned man walked over with the girl in medical attire.

"Gringo there is something you must know about us as a people. We are not uncompassionate murderers. I am going to have my island sister attend to your wounds, and you will not give her a hard time. Do we understand one another?" he asked with an intense look.

"Yes, I understand." Jonas stared at the reflection of himself in the mirror

"Afterward someone will take you to the bathroom so you can handle your business. If you keep your cool I may allow you to have sex with her." He took two steps back blocking the mirror in front and stepped toward Jonas with the gun at his side.

"Do you want to have sex with my island sister?" the dark skinned man said from the mirror standing behind Jonas. "Gringo I asked you a question!" His voice became elevated. Jonas remained silent starring at his reflection.

"No, I don't." he backhanded him again. The room erupted with laughter. Jonas felt that any sort of emotion may lead to his execution.

"Well then gringo, I leave you for now with my associates. We ask fifty thousand American for your return. A penny less I blow your brains out. Also that pretty white girl we saw you with. I have a wide imagination for her." The group of men laughed again. Jonas felt helpless. They're going kill me he thought.

The man left the room and two men followed him. His mind was racing he knew had seen a few members of this cartel out in town. He felt helpless to Jessica's safety. How would he explain to her family if something were to happen to Jess? One man across the room looked like a bar tender or even a cook from Ravens Creole, he wore similar jewelry. A large necklace of steel sun face. Jonas tried to remember what he was briefed on the ship in the event he ever were captured or knew he was being held for ransom. Best to know your surroundings but do not get caught starring or gawking at your kidnappers. Just then the man erupted with swearing in hybrid Spainish Portuguese accent pointing his finger at Jonas. The girl in scrubs pulled the man aside and spoke to him in the bathroom and then came back out to the main space. She approach Jonas and pulled a chair next to him. Her face and eyes were still covered.

She began to speak in English, "He thinks you recognize him, best not to stare or make any eye contact, ok?" "Ok then." "They really roughed you up, do you have any skin allergies to alcohol or peroxide?" "No." She took several Q tips and doused them with alcohol. The smell was very pungent. "This will sting." Jonas began to wince through his teeth. She put her hand on his leg to try and comfort him. "Señor you may or may not need stiches, I will do

19

what I can to suture your wounds. I will inform Mister X." "Mister X?" He asked. "The man who just left the room he is arranging the demands for your return to the mercy ship." She continued to clean him and wash the blood from his brown hair. "You have another gash behind your ear, I will suture." she said. "Ok, what do I call you? What is your name?" The girl just looked at him and did not respond. "Demare I," she said to the Portuguese man. He was watching the election protest on television. He grabbed a knife from the table and approached them. "Demare I'" she said again. The man pulled the knife from the brown leather sleeve and held the tip close to the neck of Jonas. Jonas did not move. The man tossed the knife to the couch and helped the girl untie Jonas. The man helped Jonas to his feet and motioned to the bathroom by the front door. The man made Jonas interlock his hands behind his head. Jonas felt a pop in torso with much discomfort, "I think I have a cracked rib" he told the girl. She looked at him and pulled her mask down. "Ok I will tend to that after you use the facilities. Also you can call me Miss Y." The Portuguese man looked at Miss Y in disgust, she rolled her eyes at him and looked at Jonas. "Don't worry about him, you can call me Miss Y." Jonas nodded.

The Portuguese man led him to the pitch dark bathroom pushing him to the middle of room where the sink was. Suddenly the light above the mirror came on filling the bathroom with blinding light, the light was buzzing loud. He shaded his eyes in his left arm. "Gringo!" the Portuguese man pounded on the door. "Gringo, you have two minutes to shit and piss that is it." Jonas looked at the sink and ran the water and drank from his hands. The smell of sulphur was nasty. "This is some bad shit I'm in." he said as he look into the mirror.

As the hours passed into that evening the noise from the streets below kept him awake. The police sirens gave him a glimmer of hope to his situation. He was exhausted, his neck began to hurt. It had been hours since he last seen Mr. X. He was now on the couch with his mouth, hands and ankles duct taped. He was hungry. The television was on in the room with a different man now watching, Jonas had not seen this man before. He too was watching the local protest coverage. The week before there was a local election and fraud suspected. Bud Guzman was not favored to win as he was not a local by birth, but did win the election. The ships security officer had briefed the aide-workers of the potential civil unrest over the next month or so.

Jonas was tired and injured. He perked up as he looked to the corner of the couch. It was the knife the Portuguese man tossed at the couch. Any sudden movement would draw attention he was nearly in the peripheral vision of the man in the room. Jonas blinked and shook his head. He thought smartly this is stupid, I am injured. I have no other choice than to let this play out. "Gringo," the man said still watching television now drinking a prestige beer. "We may be getting on the road tomorrow, you get some sleep, ok." Jonas nodded. He thought of Jessica. There were police sirens echoing in the distance.

The morning came with the red sun rising, even a partial window view was impressive given his circumstances. He was hot, sweaty and was still in pain from his injuries. Jonas sat up on the couch and glanced the room. The television was on with a topless girl in the shower, it was a television ad for body wash. You don't see that in America he thought to himself. He heard the toilet flush and then water running briefly Miss Y exited. She stood across the room with her hands on her hips looking at Jonas.

"Good Morning," she said. "Is there anything you need?"

Jonas nodded.

She came over to and removed the duct tape from his mouth. Jonas winced.

"Oh, I sorry señor." she said.

"Water? Por favor." "Si, Coming up." She replied

She walked to the television and opened a drawer and came over with a bottle of water.

"Take a breath and nod when ready I will pour some in your mouth." He did as asked. He swallowed and throat felt relief from the dryness. "More?" She asked. He nodded again.

Miss Y took a look at the couch and saw the knife in the leather cushion. She picked it up and observed it. She looked are Jonas.

"You were alone for quite a while, and you made no attempt of cutting yourself loose." she said.

She held the knife with her fist.

"Are you kidding me? I have at least a cracked rib and I can barely see. A failed escape is not worth being murdered over." he said.

"Murdered? No." she said.

"Someone would have shot you in the ass or worse your foot."

She moved to the front of the room and placed the knife in the same drawer as the water.

"You have no clue how lucky you are." she said.

"Last year this cartel killed a mechanic that was attached to a French merchant ship. You're both lucky and smart that you answered señor X smartly and then kept your mouth shut." she said.

"You are a good looking man you know, but that doesn't I want to have sex with you either." She smiled, Jonas looked at the floor then back to Miss Y and laughed.

"Yeah." He nodded.

"You don't have to respond to what I am about to say. I must say thank you for your care. I find myself less terrified with you in the room." Miss Y smiled then winked and taped his mouth.

"It won't be much longer."

She left the room as two mulatto half naked business girls came in to use the bathroom shower. They paid him no never mind.

Chapter 3

Hours had passed into the afternoon as he sat once again in solitude. He could hear arguing in the local creole off in distance. Jonas grew nervous, his heart rate began to accelerate. The arguing turned to yelling and shouting just outside the door. *Oh my God this is it* he thought. Suddenly gunfire erupted then the door was kicked open. Many port policia raided the room. Three policia came up to Jonas and secured a barrier, two more cleared the bathroom.

"Señor Parker?" A large policia man asked removing the tape.

"Yes, yes Sir, Si Señor!" Trying to catch his breath.

"We go quickly. Can you walk?" He cut and removed the tape. Jonas nodded anxiously.

They quickly led Jonas to the hallway taking an immediate left. Four doors down a woman in medical scrubs laid there it was Miss Y, she was dead of a gunshot wound. A small revolver was next to her torso. One of the men in the detail picked it up in passing. He felt shock from the sight of her blood, he kept moving with the policia feeling disbelief of what he saw. The secure group began down the stairwell. They circled the platforms down the stairwell he thought of Miss Y. He then saw the Portuguese man dead with his back against the metal railing of the stairwell. As he passed he saw the man's lifeless eyes staring at the floor. The entourage followed the exit signs. Out in the street the locals scattered at the presence of the policia. The detail filed into a white van as they sped away.

Jonas sat between two policia. He was nervous of their firearms. He was in pain with every breath he took. The large man sat in the front seat he had a chief patch on his uniform sleeve. He turned to speak as he handed Jonas a mug shot photo.

"Señor Parker did you see this man yesterday?" Jonas looked at the photo it was the dark skinned man. The words Ricardo or Rico, Ortiz, Manual and Jose were written at the bottom.

"Yes, yes he beat the hell out of me and then some." Jonas said.

"You damn lucky señor. Damn lucky." The policia said.

Jonas took notice of the policia entourage looking at one another from his comment.

"Rico is a suspect in half dozen murders across the Indies. He's Cuban, a rogue pirate."

"You're only alive because of his ransom demands. He knew you are VIP on your ship."

"I just want to go to the ship, please."

"They mentioned my girlfriend I am worried for her safety." he said.

"Señor we have been in contact with Captain McNeil, all crewmembers are present and accounted for shipboard with the exception of you. You're ships security force is on full alert.

"Señor what personal effects were you robbed of?" The chief asked.

"Just fifty gourde, why?" The chief looked at Jonas puzzled.

"Señor that is a lot of money to be caring around, you know?" Said the chief.

"The kiddos, I like to pay the kiddos for shoeshines and what not to give extra ya know." Jonas replied, the chief nodded.

"Señor we think Rico's cartel singled you out."

"What? How?" Jonas became more alert.

"Based on the ransom demands and info provided they knew you were medical personnel. This was not random, but rather planned out. If they had your medical badge or some info validating your credentials, something?"

"I don't think so, I just had the cash that's it." he said.

"Señor the ship is ahead, I come back in a few days to check in on you, I may have more info."

The van stopped at the pier. The policia stepped out and the civilian workforce became alert to them and their firearms. Jonas stepped out to the roadway, grabbing his rib cage. He took one final look at the sinister mugshot of this man Rico and handed it to the man who opened the door. He stepped forward to the front passenger door where the chief was. The chief rolled the window down.

"Chief I just wanted to shake your hand for saving my life." Jonas said.

The chief smiled, nodded his head and shook his hand.

"We were lucky with a tip from a business girl." he said.

"Señor don't mention it, we were paid well for this rescue." The chief said.

"Chief who was the woman that was killed back there in the hallway?" Jonas asked.

The Chief spoke into his radio and motioned to his driver to leave.

"Señor I have more questions and more info but I must go, we talk in a few days." As the van drove away. Jonas turned to the ship, the security force was there waiting.

-

She had been crying off and on for two days agonizing about the unknowns. A ship steward found Jessica in ships hospital changing an IV on a local.

"Doctor Adams." The steward said.

Jessica dreaded the unknown news and cringed when her name was spoken. She took a deep breath and replied.

"Yes, please God let it be good news." she said aloud.

"Yes ma'am, the Captain sends his best and wishes to inform you that your traveling companion is topside. He will require medical attention." She turned away towards the doorway.

Jessica ran up the medical stairwell skipping every other step up to the doorway to the quarter deck. She shook the door damn near off its hinges; and there he stood beaten, bruised and bloody. He was shaking the hand of Captain McNeil. She had captured McNeil's attention. The Captain turned him to his right for the couple to be face to face. They pulled towards each other near as hard as they could with tearful embrace. She kissed him over and over.

"Jess, I love you."

"I love you thank God your alive."
They both were crying holding the other.

Some of the crew members present applauded with ovation. It was an emotional reunion on the quarter deck. She led him below-decks to the hospital. The crew welcomed him back each in passing through the ship, some gave shocking looks to Jonas with his extreme bruising. The ships primary MC circuit became amplified an announcement from the Captain was about to come across bow to stern.

"This is the Captain, it is with great joy that we welcome back to Doctor Parker!" Clapping and praise rang out shipboard. The spirts were high shipboard with his return.

He sat on the hospital bed as she applied first aide to his wounds.

"Hon, who did these sutures?"

"Let's talk about it later, ok. I think I have a cracked rib."

"Jonas you don't have to talk about it, I love you."

"I love you. What's there to talk about? They tackled me, blind folded me, beat the hell out of me, drove me ten

32

minutes down the road, humiliated me for two days and even held a gun to my head and pulled the trigger." he said suddenly.

Jessica was in shock from his words. He noticed that her jaw had dropped, her blue eyes widened. "Clearly it wasn't loaded." She replied she began to cry again.

"My God my dear oh my God." she said emotionally. "You're not leaving the ship again, not even on beer night." Jessica said jokingly with tears.

"Well let's not talk loco." he said smirking. He laid back on the bed as a corpsman applied additional first aid to the side of his head. Jonas became drowsy and passed out.

It had been half a day and the ship broke schedule and went underway. At the bridge Jonas pleaded with Captain McNeil to return to the Porto.

"Sir, the policia said they would come back and question me in a few days." he said.

"Doc listen to me. Now we're under strict orders for two more medical ports. Not to mention we have no more rescue funding for policia matters."

"Sir you didn't pay the ransom?!" he questioned.

"Hell no, I would've been relieved immediately." the captain said.

"We paid twenty five hundred American from the consulate to the policia to get you back alive." the captain said.

"Sir! Sir! The chief said the cartel knew my background. The cartel mentioned Doctor Adams during my kidnapping."

"Did they mention her by name?" The Captain asked.

"No, Sir." "Ok, then. They probably saw you together out in town for drinks and dinner. You are not the first person to go through something like this." said the captain.

"Sir I apologize, my mind is all over the place. Thank you for coordinating my rescue and return." Jonas said gratefully.

"Don't thank me, thank the consulate and the bridge lookout watch. It was the lookout watch that witnessed the attack and the kidnapping." the captain replied.

"Doc you've been through hell, get some rest. Another doc showed up before lunch, he'll take over for your underway duty. The plan is to be back in Miami in twenty five days or so pending the weather report. They're tracking another possible hurricane seventy five kilos south of the Azores."

"Sir a replacement, I don't understand?"

"That rescue attempt was touch and go, I honestly thought you were dead."

Jonas sighed.

"Go below decks, I don't want to see you for at least forty eight hours.

"Yes sir." Jonas nodded and left the bridge.

He went below decks to the medical stateroom he and Jessica had been sharing. He went through his locker again and again.

"What is the matter you keep rummaging? What are you looking for?" Jessica asked.

"I don't know, something must've stood out. Jess I swear they know who we are."

"I'm telling you the policia have more info on this, they had more questions for me. I should've insisted to be left behind." Jonas was upset.

"The police chief showed me a mug shot of the guy!"

Jessica stood up and grabbed Jonas and held him by the shoulders.

"I am here, you are here. We are safe and we are leaving this place and continuing on." she said with a calm voice.

"Our jobs go on, there is more aide needed at the next two stops." she said.

Jonas tried to gather himself. "Try to be calm, you need hydration and rest."

"I don't know if this helps, but there was talk that the ships manifest may have been compromised through the consulate and port authority. They only had two on patrol pier side for security watch." She handed him a cup of ice water. He took a drink.

There was a knock at the cabin door.

"Come in," she said.

Josh Michaels had entered the room going straight over to Jonas.

"Hey champ we were beyond worried about you in Florida." Josh said.

They shook hands, Josh put his arm around Jonas.

"Hey bud, sit on the bed let me look at you." Josh insisted.

"Josh I already examined him. You men I swear, what the hell ever!" Jessica shook her head with insult.

Josh had guided Jonas to a corner bed and pulled a chair next to him.

"I know, I just want to look at his pupils for reflex."

"You both know the danger of concussions. How do you feel Jo, headache?"

"I'm more sore than anything else, Jessica wrapped my ribcage" Jonas said.

"Shake my right hand, now my left. Still got your strength, get some rest." Josh said.

"Good to see you alive my friend."

"Thanks man." "I will be in the lab." Jessica nodded to Michaels as he left.

"That's the nicest he's ever been to me." Jonas paused for a moment. "Its competition I get it." Jessica rolled her eyes to his comment.

Jonas looked at Jessica. He winced and laid on the bed. She spread a blanket over him.

"You're sick in quarters until the next port, Josh will cover you in the lab. Get some sleep."

"Jess?!"

"Yes, dear?" She stepped back into the doorway.

"Did you email or call home about any of this, the kidnapping?"

"No, not yet." she said.

"Babe, you must promise me that you won't." he said.

"I don't understand, why?" She asked.

"I don't want our friends or colleagues looking at me differently, ok?"

"Why would they do that?" She asked.

He looked at her un-patiently.

"Ok then, I promise. Love you. But you must rest, the corpsman will be in every three hours."

"Ok love."

He batted his eyes and drift off to sleep.

Chapter 4

He reached the jetty and walked half way down to be even with the tide water line. It was a month past the Fourth of July and hot as a bastard each day. He had taken advantage of those sun filled summer days with a dark tan. His work was on his mind and he was due to return, his week for night shift was starting Monday. He set up his casting rod with chunked mackerel. He opened the bail, pinched the line and casted off with authority. He loved fishing but even more the action of casting and anticipating the bite. Many beachgoers were behind him of all ages. The island was the vacation place for many people across New England and the eastern seaboard. An immediate tug on the line, a now a constant tug as he reeled and reeled and there it was a twenty two inch striper with seaweed stuffed in its mouth. The striper gleamed and shimmered from the striking sun off his circle hook. The fish thrashed on the jetty as he slipped the hook from the side of the mouth. Jonas clamped down on the fish's mouth with his thumb and the side of his index finger with his left hand under the scaly belly. He turned around to show his prize to the beachgoers and passerby's on the jetty. He admired his catch for twenty seconds and then tossed the fish back into the Gulf. This had been the best summer so far for stripe bass fishing. He loved fishing since he was a boy, there was a vast difference between fishing the Mississippi for catfish and the North Atlantic for striped bass.

He continued with another half dozen casts catching only crab. He took in the sun and the scenery mostly the boat traffic; the charters were mostly vacationers out for drinks and fishing adventure. There was a grumbling of thunder moving out to sea, lightning strikes off in the horizon up the coastline. The weather on the island can change by the moment. When the fog rolls in the temperature could drop by twenty degrees. The ocean fog is its own eclipse. Otherwise a popup thunderstorm was never out of the norm. This day was hot, a true beach day where the shallow ocean temperature truly reflects the sun.

Jonas flip flopped back to the cottage passing by his favorite set of mailboxes all uniquely themed for the beach, the seasons, nature and patriotism. He could walk by those mailboxes a hundred times and not ignore them. Jonas had thought back to Jessica's letter and began having the same feelings he had his last stint in the Caribbean. He was feeling of self-righteousness again. This is bullshit, I've done my duty and then some he thought.

Jonas knew exactly the mistake Jessica had referenced in her letter. He felt the same at times. Not long after they returned home off the ship he purchased an engagement ring. He only told Colin about it and swore him to secrecy.

"I'm serious man you have to keep this quiet, I am still thinking this out." Jonas said.

Colin nodded his head and smirked.

"You let things slip to your folks, I know you do. That's why we're having this conversation." Jonas was envious of the love and admiration that existed between Colin and his parents.

42

"Hey man listen believe it or not, mom and dad ask about you quite often. Don't get me wrong they love their sweetie pie little niece. But they asked and inquire about you and your career often. You've made quite an impression." Colin said.

"My advice to you is to hold on to this idea and not jump right in, you never know with Jessica. You could end up tomorrow morning in Montreal, that's how she rolls man."

Jonas closed his eyes and nodded, he looked to Colin.

"I know, that's why I'm in love with her."

He had moved the engagement ring two or three times since moving into the cottage. This time the ring box was clearly out of place to him. I haven't touched since I forgot it on Memorial weekend he thought. A sudden sinking feeling came over him, "Oh shit……NO!" She saw the ring!" He stepped back from the dresser, his thoughts began to race. She was expecting me to propose. It was before we left, he began to re-think the morning over and over. I had the drawer partially open prior to getting in the shower. She came in the bathroom and wanted to make love prior to leaving. He reminisced. "She knew on the way up because the drawer was open with my bag next to the dresser. Which also explains why she went ice cold on the way home." he said to himself.

He remembered that he was halfway packed and realized that the top of his dresser drawer was open where the ring box was. The box was moved forward slightly with an angle, and not firmly in the corner of the top drawer. She saw the ring box, then made her way to the bathroom as she stripped down.

She saw her ring and my bag and that's why she wanted to make love in shower before we left he thought. We never made love in the bathroom before, it was a first. She was just so happy and chatty that morning in the kitchen, packing the SUV, smiling continuously. She never was in constant dialogue she had my full attention to point where I forgot. And then it didn't happen for her.

Over Memorial Day the couple had planned a trip to the gorge in the mountains. The gorge reaches nearly one thousand feet from the base of the mountain. The granite barrier is on both sides of the step trail up. The majority of the granite is clean, pristine and cut with precision. Otherwise the granite is covered with moss giving it true New England character. The granite barrier is high nearly one hundred feet. The water is loud in mid-spring and both beautiful and captivating. Finding a moment alone was going to be a tough chore. He thought to propose at the top at just the right moment. He knew how much she loved the mountains. The couple hadn't been on get away in about a year due to their work and friend schedules. The drive up was a beautiful mountainous scene not a cloud in the sky as they drove into the sun. Indeed a beautiful day to drive up. He remembered how happy Jessica was and very chatty with an endearing mood. They held hands the majority of the way up, she was all smiles. Her light brown hair was pinned high accentuating her cheek bones. Although mid spring she was already tan. That day she wore her favorite long sleeve shirt and had her camera ready to go. She normally talked about work and her co-workers on long drives or books she was reading. When they had finally parked at their destination Jessica went to go fresh up. He stepped out of the SUV and then in sudden shock: "Oh my God I forgot the ring!"

Now she is on a ship to the West
Indies with Michaels, "Dammit." he said.

Chapter 5

Jonas Parker was born in 1970 in Rockport, Iowa apart of Alvo County near the Mighty Mississippi. His parents were working class people. His mother became the manager at the local grocery store which was walking distance to the house. His father drove an eighteen wheeler back and forth to Des Moines, he worked for himself and wouldn't have it any other way. As an only child he loved summers on the Mississippi with his mother and father, they had inherited a small family cabin up a hillside from the river just off route 22. That family cabin was the boy's entire world during his childhood. His grandfather built the cabin after he got back from the war. In the winter months at school the boy would day dream of campfires and catching big catfish at the family cabin. The boy's father taught him how to skin and fillet the evening meal fried catfish with fries, good days indeed. The boy's father took great joy in showing his son the simple joys of life. His father would take empty soda cans upstream and place them in the river as they floated pass the waterway opening of the property his son would shoot them with his .22 rifle.

"Jonas remember to keep that gun barrel pointed at the river, I don't care if you miss the cans, we're really not supposed to be doing this but the neighbors shouldn't complain."

"Yes dad." the boy replied.

"That mag holds 8 rounds take your shots calmly if you can, I know its fun to shoot." His father said.

As a boy he was covered in mosquito bites every summer. His mother would say the same thing almost weekly during those months.

"I told you Jonas to use the repellent, you're going to end up ill one of these days."

"I know mom, I know." His standard reply.

The river meant everything to the boy, he could fish right from the small beach his dad made for them. His dad also cut enough of the tree-line away to access the river without fishing line getting snagged in the limbs above. Those summer days were hot and humid always. Once a week the boy knew he could count on a passing thunderstorm. The best storms were the lightning storms that lit up the night. A sky full of connected lightning over the river was better than fireworks on the Fourth of July.

The Parkers lived in a modest three bedroom home on the outskirts of college square. The neighborhood is considered the historical side of town with civil war monuments, unique architectural style Victorian homes and the trinity cathedral church. As a boy would ride his bike and marvel at the church, the archway red doors and a stellar cross mounted at the highest point of the roof line. His father had always been taken with the precision of masonry work. Jonas was an A plus student and thrived all the way through school. He played every sport for each season, however he preferred basketball to wrestling in the winter. The boy rode his bike back and forth to school and across the neighborhoods. Everyone in town knew the Parkers. They were in good standing with the community. As many couples do they too had their share of marital drama mostly about finances. His parents loved one another and loved him very much, he was their world. His father worked like a dog. He spent many hours on the road and took on more work in 1981. His truck route expanded beyond Omaha and sometimes south to Kanas City. The boy's father was on an extended haul in August had encountered a small tornado in mid-afternoon and couldn't wait to get home to tell his son.

"Jonas I swear to you the twister was a skinny sphere of pure white hell. It was a quarter to four in the afternoon. I kept driving south as it headed north it appeared suddenly following the north bound lanes. There was an underpass up ahead with vehicles parked underneath two motorcycles and a van. I could see people making their way up and underneath for shelter as the twister spun closer and closer to them.

I couldn't believe this was right in front of me. I said God please, please be with these people.

The twister spun directly to the underpass where the people were up in the girders. Suddenly the edge of the underpass became a blur with the twister towering above. It seemed to be five seconds and then kept spinning to the next field. As I drove by suddenly there was a crack of lightning and thunder." His old man said with excitement.

"As I drove underneath the underpass I saw a man with his two little girls and two bikers slide down the concrete. The girls were crying, I sensed that nobody was hurt and I drove on." he said.

"Dad, you could've been killed. You didn't stop for shelter?" His boy asked.

His father replied; "What shelter?"

The road is where his father made his living and that as fine by him. Other than the storm event Jonas knew he could count on a phone call from father every night by 7:45 during his overnights away.

"Hey Dad." The boy enthused.

"Hey yourself pal, how was practice?" His dad asked.

"My hitting is coming along, coach says." The boy said.

"Great to hear, love ya Jo, put mom back on." He asked.

"Yes sir love you." The boy said

Jonas would always hand the phone receiver with long extension cord off to his mom as she waited patiently. The boy would run out to the backyard with the screen door slamming behind him most times. The boy noticed on one specific trip away in October that his father called back to the house every hour that night only speaking with his mother. Each time it seemed her voice became more and more agitated.

Phone at 8:45.

"What do you mean, what are you talking about?"

"I was at work, then I came home, I made dinner."

"How about yourself? You don't hear me questioning you."

Phone at 9:45

"Jim this is in your mind and doesn't exist!!"

"He is my boss and nothing else, nothing else."

"I don't care what people are telling you it isn't true."

She had ended each phone call by slamming the phone receiver on the hook violently.

At 10:45 the phone rang and rang and rang then abrupt silence in the house. At 10:50 the phone continue to ring

unanswered and then finally; stopped. The
boy heard the kitchen phone each time it
was impossible to ignore. He got out of bed
and noticed his mother was not in bed and
not in their bedroom. He walked thru the
house and found no presence of her. He
turned the outside light on and notice her car
was gone. The boy went back to bed.

The next morning the house was
silent with a note left from his mother.

Had to go out late last night to pick
up Aunt Kathy at the Elks. Her car broke
down. Be home after work. Have yourself
some cereal. Love Mom

"Aunt Kathy" was in title only. An
informality between the boy's mother and
her girlfriend Kathy Wilder who lived across
town. Kathy would watch Jonas when his
parents went out. The two were cheerleaders
through high school and graduated the same
year. The boy hadn't seen Aunt Kathy in
some time

It was Thursday morning and school
was due to start on Monday and the boy's
father was due back tomorrow. Abruptly the
boy saw his father's pickup truck pull into

the driveway. He walked aggressively into the house.

"Hey dad." The boy was happy.

"Hey sport, no mom huh?" He asked.

"No she left this note about Aunt Kathy, and then work." His father took the note for himself. "Jonas get in the truck we're going for a ride." His father was calm.

The boy's father drove out the driveway, down the alley and took a right turn towards downtown. One more right turn and they drove passed the grocery store. Funny the boy thought, mom's car isn't there. And the store looks closed. The boy noticed his father kept his eyes on the road paying no attention to the store. "Hey dad?" "Keep quiet Jonas," his father said. His father headed out of town taking route 22. They continued on down route 22 towards the sands state park. She must be with Aunt Kathy the boy thought as he watched the passing the power poles from the window as they drove on. He noticed that they were very close to the family cabin and now suddenly pulling in to see mom's car and a strange luxury car that look familiar parked side by side at the cabin. It was Mr. McCarthy's. Rick McCarthy was the owner of the grocery store where his mother worked. The McCarthy daughter was a grade above young Jonas. The truck's dual exhaust rumbled. Suddenly the boy's mother appeared from the kitchen door out the side of the house. She was in her night gown taking a step down from the deck. Strange, the boy thought. His father shut off the engine and got out, his window was down. For the first time in his life he saw his father in full rage.

"So Sara this is it, this is where we find you." he said with his arms in the air.

"Is that a question? I knew you would pull some stunt like this!" She replied with a smug look.

"I want you and that fucking weasel out of my father's cabin, now!" He demanded.

She shrugged.

"Don't you fuck with me, don't you fuck with me god dammit!!" He screamed.

"You and Kathy were caught twice last year you fucking hypocrite." As she stepped forward.

"So that's it. The note is a ruse, and you subject our son to it?! We're all done!" he said.

"Hey Jim that's fine, but just for the record we were done last year!" As she walked away slamming the door behind her.

His father took a minute to catch his breath he looked off to the river briefly and rubbed his forehead. He then faced the cabin and took a deep breath looking towards the sky. He got in the truck and drove away not looking back. It would be four months before Jonas would reunite with his mother. Jonas ended up staying with his grandmother Parker for a good period of time and eventually split the time with his mother.

After the Parkers scandal broke across town some school kids would shame Jonas for his slut mother and then his drunk dad. He had good friends during these times and into high school. Two of his best friends he could always count on were Troy Payton and Mitch O'Conner. As a boy Jonas handled anyone making fun of his family after school. He knew Troy had his back for certain if fighting got out of hand. They also walked to and from school together before their high school years. Mitch was going through a strict upbringing as he had to be home immediately after school. He just lived six houses away from the school doors. The other two boys didn't understand his family situation. At the time he had two older sisters in high school. Beverly a senior who was a wiz with numbers and knew she wanted to be an accountant. She had recently accepted a volleyball scholarship and had her path set.   Many upper classmen were interested in the O'Conner girls. Beverly had a steady boyfriend. It was Stacy who had a certain reputation. What her parents didn't know was that she took part in a sexual act with a boy and another girl for money while babysitting. The word had gotten around school that Stacy would do things for money. She had her parents convinced that she was just babysitting two blocks away on Wednesday and Thursday nights. Which was half true she was babysitting for five dollars an hour for a single mother and her daughter. One night in November of 1982 Stacy was babysitting and a boy she had previously denied at homecoming showed up at the front door. The little girl she was babysitting had already gone to bed for the night. Stacy let the boy in to watch some television. Twenty minutes later another boy showed up at the house. Before the next hour she had been tied up naked, raped several times, forced oral sex and beaten unconscious.

Luckily for Stacy little Molly McGrath knew to call 911 for help. After a month she finally came out of her coma. She missed the rest of the school year and did not return due to her injuries. The police arrested two high school seniors Kevin Fuller and Micah White both pleaded guilty and each sentenced to fifty five years in prison on several felonies. The rape and battery of Stacy O'Conner shocked the town of Rockport. Troy and Jonas made a pact to never discuss Stacy unless Mitch brought her up. It wasn't until after baseball season in 1988 until he started to talk about his sister's condition. Jonas remembered him saying that they may as well have just killed her that night. It would've been easier on his parents in the long run, especially his mother. Betty had the task of caring for her special needs daughter and her rummy husband. Frank had a tough time dealing with the sorted rumors that flew around his daughter and her assault. Betty would find him late nights in the living room sobbing. Most nights she could get him to come to bed, other nights she would leave him be. One night Frank was overly drunk and disorderly. He discharged his .38 hand gun into the fireplace multiple times screaming at the top of his lungs. The neighbors called the police thinking the worse had happened. Frank finally came out of the house and was formally brought up on charges. After which he was taken to detox.

The trio mostly played ball at Troy's house as he had the biggest yard. If they were to play basketball they went to the Parker's or Mitch's house. Going to play at Mitch's house was a last resort, but the O'Conner's loved to watch their son play with his friends. Playing ball at Troy Payton's meant interfacing his older brother Lance. Troy's older brother seemed to be content with just existing. Lance was overweight, lazy, said dumb things and had horrible grades. He had gotten a job at a local burger drive thru. His parents had grown frustrated with him. Troy would tell his friends that his dad was going to drop his brother off at military recruiting in Des Moines and drive the hell away. It was at Troy's house that the trio discovered naked women and the birds and the bees to the American cliché. This in part to the boxes of pornographic magazines Mr. Payton had collected over the years. The boys would be upstairs playing computer games and then Troy would sneak off to the basement and snag three or four sex books. Troy's dad had three tall cardboard boxes full of pornographic magazines. It was the jack pot as the trio called it. Beautiful women in various positions being very provocative with men and women. He remembered Troy being taken by a foldout of two lesbians. Most notably were the photos of women with many different breast sizes. Blonde women with huge breasts, brown haired women with fake breasts, Asian women with large and tiny breasts, black women with enormous breasts and nipples, Filipino women with huge breasts, full figured Latino women with all sort of breast sizes. There was even a five page spread of a former president seducing his secretary as he had her bent over the desk in the oval office. We flipped through porn magazines while Troy's mom would be watching soap operas or off chatting with the neighbors. He remembered Mitch opened up one magazine and a polaroid photo fell out. He showed it to Jonas. It was a nude photo of Troy's mom laying on a bed from years earlier. The two hide photo in a separate magazine to not be found again. They never told Troy about it.

Jim Parker hit the rode harder than ever before and the bottle. Twice a week his father would make an appearance distantly at baseball practice. He loved watching the boy figure the game out pitch by pitch. At times he would just watch from his truck chain smoking generic brand cigarettes. A typical trucker habit.

As a boy Jonas was a natural born leader on every team he was a part of. During football season in his junior year he had outperformed the competition from an upper classman. His team mates took notice by the lobbying of Troy and Mitch both who played on the line for offense and defense. The coach gave the starting quarterback job to the senior, simply stating in front of everyone that day in practice "That's the way it is, and that the way it goes." Coach Bowers said. Keith Bowers was the head coaches' son, and one of two captains of the team. A decent player, he had the habit of turning the ball over to the defense late in the game. The team like Keith to include Jonas. Rockport Central missed the playoffs after losing to Johnston in the late October of the fall of 1986. He finished runner up to Keith for homecoming king, which was fine by him. It was towards the end through their junior year that the trio of friends had stopped being the trio. They began to drift apart. The boys were still close on the field to include other friends and team mates. It was the combination of part time jobs, dating and a heavy homework load. Jonas was known as a studyholic.

It was graduation time for the seniors in 1987. Traditionally several juniors and seniors scope out a secluded rural area and have a keg party which is called the senior party. The Rockport senior parties were an on again off again tradition and had gained some notoriety in the county. One year there were over three hundred cars parked along Thornhaven Road leading into a wooded area known to many as Monkey Mountain. Keith Bower's mother would do what she could to find out the location and inform the police. This became her mission in life during graduation week even when she didn't have kids attending school anymore. The town council went so far as to have the sheriff come to school for an assembly of the upper classmen disparaging any such organization of obtaining alcohol, trespassing on private property and minors in procession.

"We will make arrests. You will be ticketed. You will be found liable if there were to be any sort of alcohol related accidents or injury." Said the deputy. A small gathering of friends in the middle of nowhere with few cases of beer is what took place for the next few graduating classes.

In late spring Jonas found himself leading the state in batting average as the captain of the baseball team. Troy was the most noticeable, he was jealous that he didn't get the nod from his team mates. He would address Jonas as Captain America in jest. Jonas took great pride as the leader of the team, to include his pristine uniform. His uniform fit his frame like a glove. He had grown to be nearly six feet and could run like a deer. He hit third in the batting order and made sure he led the team in runs batted in. This was exciting time as the comradery on the team spilled over into the day to day school activities. Mitch O'Conner was a great bat hitting cleanup for Rockport. Troy Payton was the catalyst of the team hitting leadoff and was a defensive dynamo in centerfield. The school hallways were wallpapered with school posters supporting the baseball team.

With his popularity Jonas was noticed by many of the young ladies at Rockport Central. He had much to offer with his fantastic grades, good looks and a good attitude. He was voted as most outgoing by his peers. Jenny Wills was very popular senior and invited him over to her house to watch a movie one day after school when her parents were at work. The two were alone in the house.

"Come see upstairs and see my room, I won't bite silly." she said smiling at him.

"Are you sure this is ok, me being here?" He cautiously walked up the stairs.

"Don't worry about it, sorry for the mess I have to share my room with my sister." she said.

He turned around in the girl's room and the two began to passionately kiss. The girl gently broke away as Jonas sat on her bed. Jenny reached behind under her sweater and removed her bra as she sat into his lap wrapping her legs around him. He was feeling and kissing her C cup breasts.

"Do you want me?" She asked.

"You have no clue how bad." He replied.

The girl sat up, pressing her breasts into his face. She reached into her back pocket displaying a condom. It looked as if it was bought from the school bathroom vending machine he thought.

"I have to tell you something;"

What's that?" he said.

"I've never had sex before." Jonas looked at Jenny. He was taken back by her statement he blinked a few times.

"I mean I've fooled around but never, you know."

"Me neither." He pressed his forehead to hers.

"Really?"

"Yes, really."

"You have to promise me some things."

"What's that?"

"Jonas you got to promise me to go slow." "Alright, I promise."

"And you have to promise not tell anyone." she said quietly.

"Scouts honor, I promise."

Chapter 6

The cottage on the island was a two bedroom, the guest bedroom had been converted into a small office. It happened to be full of Jessica's hoarding. Text books stacked along randomly along the walls. Her crafts and sewing material laid out in no planned order although what seemed to be mid-project. Jessica's handed down old hope chest was against the back wall. The antique was a dark chocolate color with two replacement legs on opposing sides oddly the same color of the cedar shingles of the cottage. Jonas thought it was at least one hundred years old. Folded a top we're several old hand made knitted blankets; hand me downs from her aunts in Nova Scotia. Jonas stood in the door way with his arms partially extended across the door way taking in the room of her effects, taking a deep breath and exhaling slowly. He read the letter from Jessica again. In the end she says that she is sorry, she rarely apologies to me or anyone for that matter. From the kitchen he heard his cell phone buzzing off the white granite counter top. Jonas became alert to the contact display 'AW'.

"Hello."

"Hello yourself mister." A familiar voice sounded.

"Ashley Winters, what have I done now?" Jonas lit up.

"You're guilty of going fishing today without inviting me along, nice striper by the way." she said.

"You saw that, huh?! Thankyou."

"Michelle and I we're laying out, you had some fans on the beach giving you the thumbs up."

"Hey good times with good people; the summer slogan of 2001." he said in jest.

"How bout; Wicked hot in more ways than 2001." She replied. Jonas heard background laughter from her twin sister Michelle.

"Nice. When did you get in town?" He asked.

"Last night, late. The traffic up from Boston was horrible I had wine with my mom when I got in." she said.

"Colin says you've been self-isolating, that is not healthy Jonas." "I know." he said.

"So uh, what's going on tonight? Going to Colin's?" she asked.

"Yeah, fairly certain he is expecting me. I'm just not sure if I'm in the mood for tequila." he said.

"I know that feeling, have you at least heard from Jessica?" she said.

"Five days ago. She also penned me a letter, I feel like I've been dumped unofficially." he said.

"I'm sorry Jonas, this leaving spur of the moment is too erratic, isn't it?"

"Yeah, well, she took a phone call eight or nine days ago from a colleague of ours for this mercy mission to the West Indies. She halfheartedly asked me to go with her, but she knows I can't bail on the hospital. She was booked on flight for the following evening." He explained.

"Who is the colleague?" she asked.

"Friend of ours Josh Michaels, he's was in town over the Fourth for drinks we had a goodtime."

"Really?"

"Yeah, Ashley I know how it looks but I got to give Jess the benefit of the doubt on this." he said.

"Well then. I guess that's that, so we'll see you tonight?"

"Yeah, nine thirty or so good bye for now."

"Roger that." He closed his phone.

Jonas began to pick up the living area he made his way to the bedroom and took a look around. She left one hell of mess for me to clean up he thought. Papers, clothes, bed linen and shoes were scattered. He grabbed the bathroom trashcan and began to gather what he deemed was of no use. There was a thin piece of white plastic in the trash. Jonas dumped the trash on the floor and picked up the item. "A pregnancy test?!" he said aloud. Jonas went out to the living room and sat on the couch. He put the test on the coffee and stared at it. The test indicated a double red line for a positive result. He didn't know what to think, how to feel. For a moment he felt numb, and pictured her back in the library years prior. Jonas began to do the math to the last time he and Jessica had been together. Between their work and friend schedules it had been since Memorial Day.

Is she running from me and the test results?

Or is she running to someone else with the test results?

He shook his head. She's been vulnerable since Memorial Day. She is hurting and she called Michaels that's why he was here for the Fourth.

He felt a feeling of betrayal. Her leaving is an omission of guilt in his mind.

Chapter 7

Jonas walked Beach Plum
Avenue. The sunset behind him reflected
how hot it was this day in a red haze across
the sky behind. He thought of similar
sunsets on hot days growing up, the sky
behind him looked to be on fire. Jonas felt
mixed emotions. She clearly took off with
Michaels after what the test results reveled
he thought to himself. He kept on towards
Sanderson Manor as he called it, not far
from the cottage which was convenient after
drinks. The mansion was on the biggest lot
on the island. Their residence was at the end
of the avenue which also dead ended to a
beach fenced walkway to the ocean. Each
house lot was wood fenced mixed with
blooming beach roses. As he approached the
beach roses became mixed with high swale
grass. The Sanderson's private drive is
well- lit off the avenue slightly curved up to
the wide circle driveway.

The lawn is crisp and freshly cut
almost daily, same as was the shrubbery that
lined every outside walkway. The back of
the mansion faced the Atlantic with a private
guest house out in the back. George recently
had contractor build veranda on the back of
the home the ocean view was indeed

striking. The house was a well built two story cape with a series of bump-outs and gabled rooflines that extended out into the back. The home has an attached three car garage that faces back up the avenue. Above the garage is a finished space and is where Colin resides when there is company on extended stay. The exterior of the home has perfectly tanned cedar shingles which lined every vertical surface including the outside buildings. The mansion has a series of skylights front to back to include dozens of windows all with thick white trim making the cedar shingles pop with the intensity of the sun. The home has three stone fireplaces for each wing but the staple was the grand fireplace in center of the home for entertaining. The mansion is built on five acres with six bedrooms and six full bathrooms, a perfectly groomed backyard with the essential summer amenities of an outdoor bar, in ground pool with a side hot tub. Colin kept the ping pong table setup all summer long, it tended to double for drinking games. Mary would voice her disapproval at times.

Off the beach path was the low tide which unveiled a wide spread of rocks which formed into the ocean at a ninety degree angle. This rock formation created several standing pools of water on the beach about a hundred yards or so towards the jetty. Every year the vacationing children would gather bucket by bucket from the tide pools and build there in the sand. The parents would watch from their beach chairs, drink and soak up the hot sun.   The island provided the perfect family summer for most.

Beach towels draped the outside the bone white banisters miscellaneously around the mansion. The Sanderson's home had a museum feel it just seemed to grow as you walked through. The kind of home you felt proud to be associated with even though it belonged to another. That's the way Jonas thought of it and never lost that feeling since his first invitation.   Colin had told Jonas that his parents never traveled for the holidays. All relatives came to them and stayed with them Mary would not hear of it otherwise. Mary and George Sanderson kept to their routine. They only traveled to Stowe for a week of skiing in February each year. Colin primarily stayed in the guest house out back, he was the youngest of three. His brother and sister were off with their own families locally. The Sanderson's were the socialites of envy on the island. They are the uncontested power couple in town. Both George and Mary were involved in every town committee, rotary club and chaired the island resident meetings. The island status quo carries a certain perception is reality feel amongst the residents. The common opinion turned into a common island cliché regarding George and Mary "it must be nice."

There were plenty of people parked in the circle drive. Jonas walked past Ashley's sports car. He noticed a sticker on the back windshield. The depiction of a dancing native playing a flute set a care free mood and was a perfect description of Ashley. Up the slate walk way he let himself in the thru the glass doors. Just before nine thirty and there were a few hundred people gathered with drink in hand. The house vibe was high, the house speakers rang out with a jazz and trumpet mix. Jonas waved, shook hands and made greetings with the neighborhood regulars. A good many were from out of state, friends of the family renting on the island. Jonas attested to what Colin said on the beach earlier that day there were a lot of women present at the house. However what Colin forgot to mention was the eye popping cleavage that was on display. There was an easy rule to follow when it came to women busting out with intent. Briefly look and try not to get caught glaring. The regulars knew who Jonas was and when asked about Jessica he briefly mentioned her work schedule to avoid further questioning. He caught Mary's eye as he walked through the grate room. She was with company.

"Jo, wonderful to see you babe." Mary is all smiles with a glass of Riesling.

"Hi Mary. How's your day?"

"Amazing! Hit the back bar, Colin should be bartending"

He made his way out the back deck as George was making his way probably for marching orders.

"Jonas my boy, you look great!"

George approached with arms extended shaking hands then a brief hug.

Jonas was thought of like family to them. He felt odd of what details George and Mary could know about Jessica's abrupt departure.

"This is the last big shindig for the month, so make this one count." He pointed to Jonas.

"George you said that last month."
The two men laughed.

"I know, I know. I have to keep a
happy shop with Mary. You know." He
smiled.

"No doubt, I see Colin is hard at it.
Sir get a drink later?" Jonas asked.

"Let's try. I tend to get busy with
saying good bye to folks, Mary's rules."

George began to break away.

"The drinks are out back Jonas." He
motioned to his son.

Colin was bartending out back with
Michelle they had just broke away from
kissing. Colin and Jonas pointed at each
other for acknowledgment. Colin pointed at
two seats at the bar. Jonas looked to him in
confusion.

"Hello Jonas my boy, love your
shirt." He looked to his left. Ashley stepped
closer and placed her arm around the side of
him they both laughed. They kissed each on
the cheek. They stood together hip to hip
looking to one another. He was taken back
by her beauty. Her sandy blonde hair, tan
slender build, blue eyes. Beauty was not her
only feature. Ashley was working towards

making partner at a Boston law firm but took a modified roll recently.

"What do you mean you're not interested in becoming partner anymore? That's shocking to hear." The two were sitting at the bar.

"I'm done working seven days a week ten and twelve hour days. Done." She leaned in.

"The firm is very high school with people snitching left and right doing whatever they can to get ahead, its crap. Another thing, I'm not dating anyone from work ever again it doesn't work." she said.

Colin and Jonas briefly caught one another's eye.

"So what is this the new roll?" Colin asked. He gave them both a gin and tonic.

"We have clients that find themselves in need of help behind the scenes. I work with two other people where we find the legal loopholes. Let's leave it at that." she said smiling with a slight laugh.

"You're a fixer?" Colin said.

"Well that didn't take long to figure out." Ashley replied taking a drink. Michelle laughed.

"What do you mean a fixer?" Jonas asked.

"Clients don't want their dirty laundry aired out in public, especially if there are being extorted. It's one thing to advise a client out of hit and run involving prescription meds. But when someone's reputation is about to be ruined for a million or two million dollars that's a whole other. I get paid well and get to see mom more often."

"And here is to my drunk twin sister woo hoo!" The girls high fived.

"Who's the drunk?" Michelle said laughing.

"Colin." Michelle nudged him. He looked at her. "Mother Mary." she said.

Mary had suddenly walked up from the beach path with guests.

"Ok then I see the usual suspects have found one another. Colin honey, we have some people leaving that we should walk out, bring Michelle and make the introduction. I need this donor for the

78

library. Take a shot of water." Mary walked away, Colin nodded.

Michelle looked at Ashley and took a deep breath. Ashley handed her a small bottle of eye solution.

"Work and play, right? I'll rave about her dress." Michelle said.

"It may take more than that, you know what to do. Just like last night I will complement the new car. Phil was on the wait list for nearly a year for that shit box." Colin was growing tired of playing the role of a phony host. Especially with his peers around. They know the real him.

"You're quite the fixer." Jonas said.

"Stop." Colin rebutted.

They left the bar and headed up the deck stairs. Colin and Michelle were good when they wanted to be. Colin's commitment to a forever relationship was still not present to Michelle.

Ashley hopped off the bar stool and headed behind the bar. She grabbed a half empty bottle of tequila and looked at Jonas.

"Let's go for a walk. It's a full moon." she said.

"You're the boss."

They walked the sand path for about minute with party goers coming back from the beach. They reached the white sand hot from the day the stood and took in the waves. The waves sparkled from the moonlight and gleamed. Ashley took a drink from the bottle and passed it Jonas. He did the same. They began to walk down toward the water in the bright moonlight. Ashley suddenly slipped on the wet sand getting her bottom wet, she laughed. He enjoyed her.

"Oh my god you're too funny. At least you didn't spill the booze." he said. "Up we go." Ashley sprung up wrapping her arms around Jonas and kissed him. They kissed long.

"I've been waiting for that all day." she said.

They took in one another with the moonlight.

"That's the nicest thing to happen to me in a month." he said.

"How do you feel, hurt?" The moon was bright her eyes were locked on his.

"I don't think so. Some things have come to light." he said.

"What do you mean? Has something happened?" She asked.

"Ashley what I am about to tell you is top secret. I think Jess is pregnant with his child. I think she's thinks the same. Given her leaving on mission with Josh Michaels."

"Wait a minute, why do you think Jessica is pregnant? Why does she think that?" Ashley asked.

"I was cleaning today and found a used test. It was positive." he said.

"Whoa! Jo you talked about giving the benefit of the doubt. The benefit has left the building." Her tone was elevated.

She handed the bottle over to him. He looked at the moon and turned to the ocean and he took a prolonged swig and let out a deep breath.

"Ashley I needed to get that off my chest." Giving the bottle back to Ashley she took a shot.

"Ok then." he said.

She leaned into Jonas and they kissed again he felt the softness of her body pressed up against his. She kissed with the intent of romance pulling him towards her.

The ocean washed as they kissed. The two broke away now forehead to forehead.

"Colin, Michelle and I saw them together when you were on shift over the fourth."

"What? Define together?" He insisted as he brought his head up looking at her with seriousness.

"Walking on the beach close like we are now. Mary notice of them too." she said.

"Mary was making her way through the house and asked what had our attention, she looked confused by them and gave a very hard look."

"Ash, it's been rocky. She was expecting me to propose over Memorial Day but." She stopped him.

"It's nearly midnight we could go back the party or we could go back to your place." she said.

"We have to go back to the party. You know how they are about formalities." Jonas said.

"Let's go back and when you hear me say the words 'second shift' you fake a cell phone call and meet me out front." he said.

She looked at him in question. "It'll work. Trust me." he said.

They held hands as they walked the beach back together. The ocean lightly crashed as the moon was full.

There were a few partiers up from the beach path.

They walked thru the bar area, there was a couple together at the fire enjoying the ambience.

Jonas approached the couple, "Hey man have you seen Colin or Michelle?"

"Out front, I think. It has been a little while. Mary and George may have gone to bed."

Jonas was feeling a good buzz, but had the ability to keep politeness a priority with the many folks around.

They took a look around and didn't recognize the remaining guests' some were walking down the driveway calling it a night. Jonas looked through the front and noticed only Ashley's car. Ashley was reading the room for familiar people.

Jonas looked to Ashley.

"You're looking at me a certain way. You never know whose watching." she said.

Jonas looked at her and smiled. "Agreed, second shift." he said.

She smiled and held out her cell phone.

Chapter 8

They were nestled together naked with only a sheet over them. His arm draped over her. The girl slept easy. He couldn't stop staring at the digital clock. A brief thunderstorm was passing, it rang loud over them. The lightning lit up the bedroom, the rain was heavy then soft. It sounded of small water drops hitting the roof.   It was five forty five, he thought random thoughts from the past. He thought back to his time in the Indies, the hot sun and humidity. The good people that were that ship's crew. He thought of the poker nights at sea. He thought of having ice cream with Jessica on the mess decks after leaving the final port and how sore was still at that time. He thought briefly of his capture, mostly of his caretaker. He thought more about his absentmindedness over Memorial weekend. We never really talked about getting married he thought, we never talked about children. Maybe I was just caught in a moment of content. Ashley rolled over into his chest.

"You're not sleeping." she said softly.

"The storm. You're not sleeping either." He lightly rebutted.

"I was out for an hour or so. I love the suddenness of a thunderstorm." She yawned. They were now laying looking at the ceiling taking in the flash of lightning.

She then moved again and stretched her body now laying back into him,"What was it like being abroad?" She asked.

"That's funny you ask, I was thinking about floating on that tin can a few minutes ago."

"You certainly came back with your share of scars." She kissed his neck.

"Yeah, you know it was good. You meet some really awesome people."

He scratched the side of his head.

"You also meet some shitty people ya know." He took a deep breath.

"Yeah but that's everywhere." she said.

"Well in general. I would always try to go out in town, or the Port-o as the locals refer and hit a local beach watering hole. Everyplace we stopped there is a slew of them on every beach walking path almost

86

every two hundred feet or so. A lot of the same look of bamboo and tiki decor or a nineteen fifties theme showcasing James Dean or Elvis. The port-o sidewalk on the beach is a wave of black slate opposed by a wave of white slate. The waves are wide then skinny all the way up and down the sidewalk.

I always have a beer or mixed drink and tip the bartender generously. Tipping the bar tenders goes along way especially if you need a cab late night. One of the bartenders brought her little brother to the ship for medical attention once. He had a nasty gash on the top of his thigh it required stiches but they waited too long and gangrene was setting in. She told me he tried to jump a metal fence. He was probably on the run that's how it is sometimes."

"What did you do for the boy?" She asked.

"Irrigated the wound and gave him antibiotics. I make the patients comeback for the pills."

"Why?" She asked.

"If I give them a bottle of pills they will sell them instead of taking them, they need the money."

"I just couldn't imagine living like that." she said.

Ashley sat up looking at Jonas. She took his hand.

"What? You look like you want to ask me something." he said.

"I do. But I don't want to overstep my bounds, sensitive ya know." She replied.

"Geez Ashley I've practically spilled my guts to you over the last day." He sat up and looked at her. There was a flash of lightning.

"What is it?" "Ok then."

"I feel like you know more about this whole thing than what you're really letting on."

"What, what are you talking about?"

"What is the real backstory with this Josh Michaels?" She asked looking to him.

Jonas shook his head rolling his eyes.

"You know him well, not randomly?" She asked.

"Yeah, he always led the study groups back in school. Funny dude."

"Jess introduced me to him. He always had a new girlfriend by the month. We double-dated to parties or social events."

"Colin said that he was on the ship with you." she said.

"Yeah he filled in the last month home, he was on emergency standby."

Ashley looked at him for more info. She was easy to read.

"Ok. I suspected two years ago that they had gotten together, they happened to both be in New York at that time. We were due for a break. It was tough dialing into one another and carrying the burden of a long distance relationship. At that point we were on two different paths."

"You seem to have found plenty of logic in all at." Ashley said.

He looked at Ashley, she smiled at him.

"Wow you can really read me. Ok. There was a nurse practitioner that I went out with for a period of time." He explained.

"Hey wait, I've watched you juggle suitors on the island last year. What about you and what's his name, Karl?" Jonas questioned.

"Completely different Jo."

"How?" he said in jest.

"Karl was a work fling with benefits, kept on the down low. In fact we pretended to hate each other in front of people to throw them off and I wasn't in love with him."

He gently squeezed her hand and let go.

"I will not to be saying that word for a while." he said.

"So what were circumstances for calling a doctor on emergency standby on an underway mission?" She asked.

"Coffee?" He asked then got out of bed. Lightning flashed lighting up the room.

"To early for coffee. Where are you going?" She asked.

He turned around standing in the doorway starring at the floor.

Ashley became more serious.

"Why did the ship call for Josh Michaels in on emergency standby?" He stood straight and looked at Ashley.

"Be direct with me." Her tone was serious.

"The ship thought I was dead, ok. Or soon to be dead."

"What!?"

"I was kidnapped for thirty six hours."

"Oh my, how horrible!" She got of bed and went to him.

Jonas put his hands out and held her at her shoulders. He shook his head.

"No, stop. That is the reaction that I don't want."

"What, why?"

She put her hands together and pressed them against her lips.

"Ashley I can deal with my scars. Ok?"

"I don't understand." she said.

"What I can't deal with is people looking at me differently knowing that."

"Ok, ok then. I will keep to myself. Jonas I am here to talk."

He looked at her and smiled and kissed her cheek and felt her hair.

"I hope we can talk after the sex marathon you put me through."

They laughed and embraced on another.

"I need a coffee." he said.

"I need something else." She pulled him back to bed.

The sun rolled through the bedroom and was now shinning on his face and he woke. The display on the clock was blinking 915. He was alone in the bedroom.

"Ashley, Ash."

"Yo, where did you go?"

He walked into the kitchen.

"Ice Coffee?" She handed it to him.

He sipped from the straw it felt like a shot of life.

"Delicious, thank you." he said.

"You're out of creamer by the way."

"You left huh?" He asked.

"I had to check on my parent's house mom went to the cape, I showered there."

"You have me thinking of something you said earlier."

"You said that you met some shitty people abroad, how so?"

"You really want to hear this?" He asked.

"Jonas, I've only vacationed in the Bahamas with my family like once. You've experienced the realism of these places. she said then sipped her coffee.

"Alright then. These are the third world countries where the majority of the children fight for scraps. I was outside on the deck of a restaurant and I saw some kids fighting in the street over something in the dirt roadway. I thought what the hell could be so valuable in the street. I then turned to my right and saw some of the ships security force were tossing coins in the street watching the kids fight over the money. Clearly not an act of charity but rather to watch children fight for entertainment. I overheard two of them taking bets on which kid could beat down the other. Some of the children were in tears. Some of the older girls were the toughest." He scratched the back of his neck.

"If the private companies who fund these missions knew of this kind of stuff there would be hell to pay."

"That's crap, did you turn them in for that?"

"No I didn't." "That's shitty too. It's just going to happen again on the next mission" she said.

"No doubt." He replied with no hesitation.

He began to stare off in in space.

"I'm afraid or maybe it's just anxiety." he said.

"Of what?" Her attention peaked.

"Nothing, forget it." He felt embarrassed and didn't mean to say that out loud.

He could hear his cell phone buzzing from the bedroom.

"What's the plan for the day?" He asked her. "I gotta find Michelle before I can answer that, but I will be laying out later."

"She didn't answer her cell. I'm going to stop in at Colin's." Ashley walked over to the fridge. She pulled a container from her bag.

"Half and half, right?" "Yes, thank you."

She took two steps towards him. He looked down at her blue eyes, tan face and blonde streaky hair.

"So let's go back to last night when things were top secret on the beach." He looked at her oddly.

"Yeah. What about it?"

"In theory you could be the father, right?" she said.

"You're not going to put me on the witness stand this morning, are you?" He said.

He moved across the kitchen and folded his arms he looked to the floor and then to Ashley. "Yeah, I guess so it's a long shot it's been nearly been seven and half weeks since the last time. I am pretty certain she had her cycle since our last time."

Ashley nodded her head and looked at him curiously.

"I am an honorable man Ashley. If it's my child then it's my child. The child did no wrong." he said.

"You know Jonas, you are indeed one of the good ones."

He smiled and then abruptly turned his attention to the bedroom. His phone was buzzing again. She stepped towards him.

"So uh, what is this thing here between us?" She pressed her breasts up against him.

"To be honest I haven't thought of a definition for it. But you have my full attention."

"Good answer. I have to find Michelle. I will let you know about laying out." She kissed his lips and headed out through the sliding door. Jonas let out a sigh.

Chapter 9

It was nine forty five at Sanderson Manor with the speaker system activated.

"Collie." His father's voice rang out. Colin went to the speaker.

"Sir."

"Tell Michelle coffee is up, stuff she bought."

"Waffles too." Mary said from the background.

"Thank you," Michelle said from the bed. She draped her arm over her forehead.

Colin was wrapped in towel just out of the shower.

"Just call me a womanizer then, if that's how you see me." Colin said.

"What?!" The speaker rang out loud it was still activated.

"Shit, sorry." He hit the switch to off.

"Nice now they know were up here arguing." Michelle said.

"I'm not arguing."

"I didn't call you a womanizer. You come across very much inviting the attention."

"What the hell are you talking about?" He shook his head at her.

"I have make nice to the daughters of these high profile people as they rub their boobs on you. You had your arm wrapped around Hailey Martin for over a minute." Michelle said in frustration.

"Yeah, I felt your glare that's why I stepped back to get the wine." He explained.

"I'm just playing the part and being polite. We were all chatting around the kitchen island, you we're included and a big hit." Colin said.

"Colin you know that stuff bothers me and you never shy away from it." Her tone was emotional.

He sat on the bed. He had true feelings for Michelle.

"I am not going to be your summer fling. You seem to avoid introducing me as your girlfriend."

She had gotten dressed and headed for the bathroom walking passed him. He grabbed her hand and pulled her tight to him.

"That's enough. I won't hear any more of this. It's my fault, it won't happen again. I'm sorry." He held her.

They we're in love with one another. But neither would say it.

Michelle began to well up with tears. He held her soft face and kissed her.

"I just don't want to be someone that you became infatuated with and then that's it."

"Stop." he said.

"I mean it. Last night won't happen again."

They held each other. They felt lucky to have found one another.

He looked at her. "I'm in love you. Do you know that?" He asked her.

She put her forehead on his chest. "I'm in love with you too." she said emotionally.

"But these social gatherings bring on pressure, like a job interview. It's a lot."

"They're only temporary and you handle them first class, you're a big hit babe."

"Do your parents really like me?"

"The real question is do you like them?" he said in quick response.

"Not everybody does." he said.

The speaker became activated.

"Ok then, in one minute I am sending Mary up." His father's voice rang out. Michelle started to break away.

"Wait let me throw on some clothes and will go downstairs together."

She checked herself in the bathroom mirror. She was indeed an identical to Ashley.

Michelle was outgoing and independent. Her career had taken her to Seattle then to San Francisco then to New York and then back to Boston. She always seemed to be in the right place at the right time for changing positions. She had waffled on a job in Arizona. She knew she had to come home last year. She was good with clients and managing high net worth assets in the financial markets. She had made her parents proud and missed her mother dearly. The twins lost their father last year. Their mother was still leaning on family on the cape.

He shuffled himself following Michelle down the winding stair case. Mary met them at the bottom.

"Good morning Michelle, sleep well?" Mary asked greeting her with arms out.

"Excellent as always, thank you." Michelle made her way toward the kitchen.

"You look fabulous." "Thankyou." she said briefly turning around.

Mary became tight lipped and glared at her son.

"Good Morning Mom."

"Good Morning." She nodded and stared at him.

"We need to speak later in private." Her tone was serious.

"Mom." "Later. I said." She continued on and he followed her to the kitchen.

Mary turned away from him. Colin looked at the floor tile with a quick sense of shame.

Mary was wearing heels they echoed with authority down the hall. Heels on a Saturday morning never a dull moment. He thought.

"Damnit I burnt the coffee." George said. "It was three minutes or two? I'm sorry my dear."

"No, no it's perfect. The stronger the better." Michelle let him off the hook.

George's cellphone began to ring.

Michelle checked her cell, "Oh I missed a call from Ash." she said.

"Good Morning Phil." George left the kitchen. Mary was interested to the call as she watched him leave the room.

"So what's the plan? It's gonna get hot again today with another possible late thunderstorm." Mary said.

"My sister should be here shortly, even away mom still has errands for us to get done. But I will take a waffle with whipped cream."

Colin sat at the table. "Ashley is on the scene." he said.

Mary waved for her to come in. Ashley was about to ring the bell. She made her way in to the kitchen.

"Young lady no need for that, you're practically family. Good Morning by the way."

"Thank you Good Morning to you." They hugged. Colin smiled at Michelle.

"There's coffee." Colin said to Ashley. "All set, thanks." She kissed her sister's cheek and sat next to her.

"Hey love." "Hey." Michelle responded.

"You know I am glad we are all in the house together again it has been a few weeks. Being busy with all the craziness of the functions and all." Mary said.

Mary moved to the front of the kitchen table.

"I've been kicking myself for not bringing this up at the time. But do any of you know who that man was that day?"

"Mom, what man, which day?"

"The man walking close with Jessica on the beach that day over the holiday."

The three of looked at one another. Michelle shook her head slightly side to side as did Ashley.

"A friend of hers I guess, I've never met him." Colin said.

"It was an odd scene. Friends don't walk together like a couple." Michelle said.

"Agreed." Ashley said.

"Exactly. Great minds think alike." Mary looked at the girls.

"Colin I told your father I woudn't mention this but I don't care I am too bothered by it.

We saw them kissing at the spot and then abruptly going off into the cottage."

"Mom, timeout. How do you know where 'the spot' is?" Colin smirked and then looked to Michelle and Ashley.

"I've chased three kids around this island partying and what not. I know what I'm talking about." The four of them shared in laughter.

The spot is a semi make out area between the old tennis courts and a wooded area close to the cottage. You could get a full view of who was at the spot from Shelby Lane. Mary and George had friends who lived on Shelby.

"We had lunch with at the Martin's and we saw them in plain sight." Mary took a drink of her coffee.

"Monica told me she saw them making out days earlier. Conveniently when Jonas was on shift. And now she has suddenly taken off on mission with this man!?"

"What!?" Colin and Michelle both blurted out.

"So much for keeping this information low key." George stepped into the kitchen removing his hat.

"Morning Ashley." "Good Morning, ya know we should get going." Ashley looked to Michelle and stood up.

"Right, right that's right." Michelle agreed and nodded to the idea.

"I'll walk you out." Colin said looking back towards his parents oddly.

"You two girls come back later, ok. If you call you mother tell I said hello." Mary said.

"Ok then." Michelle said.

Mary smiled. Colin look to his mother. She became tight lipped and looked away.

George smiled and was pleased at the sight of Colin with Michelle Winters.

They gathered their belongings, Colin opened the door for the girls as they all walked out to the walkway.

"That was a bomb, I didn't expect." Colin said.

"Colin. There is a lot more to this with your cousin. Alot." Ashley said.

"What? How do you know stuff? he said.

Where did you end up last night?"

"Is that really what's on your mind? I'll never tell." she said.

Ashley opened the car door.

"Says the fixer." Colin said jokingly.

"Oh, my God." Ashley sat in the car slightly shaking her head.

She put on her sunglasses.

He pulled Michelle close. "Do I get to see you later?"

"I don't know, I got a lot of stuff to do…." She look at him and smiled.

"You'll know where to find us at two thirty." She kissed him.

"So I guess this means were official. An item?" He asked.

"I don't know, you seem, shaky?" She laughed.

"You're gonna make me eat crow." He replied.

"Ha. Yes. An item we are. I get a ring right?" She winked at him.

Colin smiled, he was happy. "If you play your cards right."

"Come on, you should've gotten enough last night. We gotta go Michelle."

"See ya." Michelle got in the car. They drove away.

Chapter 10

Colin walked in down and back through the kitchen. His father was having his coffee at the kitchen island with his head in the morning paper. Colin grabbed an energy drink and walked toward the back deck.

"Stop." His mother's voice from the above walkway.

Colin turned around. He put his drink on the island and looked up.

"I know mom the speaker. I am sorry, totally my fault."

She was making her way down the staircase. Her footsteps were loud.

Colin thought of a host of issues that he knew his parents were displeased with. One of which was not being as personable as he could be with certain guests.

"That's not entirely it." she said.

"Where is this going with Michelle?" Mary was direct.

"Wow. That's the first time you've ever asked me a question about a girlfriend of mine, do you realize that?" he said defiantly.

"We feel we have the right to know given the recent passing of her father. What is that a problem or something?" His mother was also defiant.

"No. But you really think of me as a love 'em and leave 'em kind of a guy don't you?"

His parents looked at one another.

"We're concerned for the girl, we're concerned for you." His mother said.

"You're getting to be a little too old to be having these flings, don't you think?"

"If you have a problem with her, just tell me." Colin's voice was elevated.

His father put his hand out.

"To the contrary. We love Michelle. We like the idea of two together. She is engaging, bright, educated, successful and very well mannered. Given all that both girls and their mother still seem depressed since John's passing."

His father leaned over the kitchen island.

110

"What we would like, is for people to know that you're in a relationship."

"And off the market." His mother blurted out with her arms crossed. George looked at his wife.

"As opposed to what being out on the prowl?" Colin said jokingly.

George raised his brow.

"Be serious with us. Ok. This conversation could be a game changer for you."

"Just relax. I probably should wait until Michelle is here to share this. But we have discussed our feelings. We are in love and committed." he said then giving a delayed smile.

Mary stepped forward to her son she looked to her husband and smiled.

"Really! You have, you are! That's wonderful to hear. Wonderful, wonderful."

Mary hugged Colin. "Oh, I love you and her. Exciting."

"Now can we discuss the five hundred pound elephant in the room?" Colin said.

"How do you know Jessica ran off with Josh Michaels?"

"How do you know is name?" His parent said at the same time.

Colin put his hands up. "I asked first."

"She made a reservation using her parent's landline as a backup for confirmation. Patty immediately phoned us - how did they mistake the name Josh for Jonas. She thinks the whole thing is a big mistake.

Chapter 11

Jonas starred at the indication of voicemail on his cell phone. He began to listen.

"Jonas this your mother, you need to call me Jonas. It's your father he is not well. I love you call me." His mother sounded more troubled this time than the last. He called her.

"Hello."

"Hi mom."

"Hi Jo, I need a favor. I need you to come home." she said immediately.

"Does he need rehab again mom?" He asked.

"Jonas your father has lung and pancreatic cancer." she said bluntly.

Jonas sat on the bed and closed his eyes. His heart began to race. Almost five seconds had passed. He cleared his throat and let out a deep breath.

"Hospice?"

"Yes, through Renee, he has a bed at the nursing care center. You remember Rick's daughter Renee don't you?"

"Yes mother I know who she is." His voice became annoyed.

"Oh, ok. We are all very proud of you sweetie I mean it."

"Thankyou."

"We haven't seen you in quite some time, your father mentioned you on a ship in the Caribbean and also living with a young lady."

"Not really anymore mom, but there is someone. A good someone."

"Oh good to hear honey. Good. You are more than welcome to stay with us or you can stay at your fathers. Will you be coming home alone?" She asked.

"I'm not sure mom. I need to make some phone calls."

"Ok honey. Listen they have your father in state of illusion with the drugs. It is not easy to take."

"I know the cause and effects mom, I will call you when I get there."

"Ok honey. We checked the other day and your father's house key is still hidden in the same spot. I am very sorry about all this. I love you."

Jonas felt himself begin to well up again. It was the sound of his mother's voice that began to really get to him. The comfort that it used to give him from childhood started to fill him up with emotion.

"Me too. Bye." He closed his phone and cried. He sat in the cottage alone thinking of how many ways he was a bad son for not communicating or taking the additional time to see his father over the years. He thought of fishing at the cabin beach with his father and playing catch with him. The simple pleasures of youth and the joy they had brought even for a brief time. "That's life." he said aloud.

Chapter 12

The twins drove down the Sanderson's private drive. Then out and right on Beach Plum avenue.

"Hung over oh my." Michelle lit a cigarette and leaned the seat back.

"Me too. Really Michelle leaning the seat back we're like five minutes from mom and dad's." Ashley said.

"Finally I get a cigarette. His family is great but the formalities are a bit much. Mary saw me smoking in the car when got there last night."

"Did she say anything to you about it?"

"No, I tried to hide it. She just looked the other way, but I know she saw me. She would consider herself as being rude by saying something about it. I'm sure Colin will get an earful about it."

Michelle sat up.

"So, how did that go last night?"

Ashley kept her eyes forward briefly glancing over at her sister.

"Gimme a drag." The two exchanged the cigarette back and forth. Michelle took a hard look at her sister.

"Please tell me you didn't." Michelle said. Ashley approached the four way stop then turned and smirked at her sister. Michelle looked forward and closed her eyes.

"No Ash, no. Tell me you didn't sleep with him. I was hoping you were just joking back there with Colin. Ashley the guy is in a relationship with my future in-laws niece. How could you do this to me?"

Ashley pulled in the driveway and parked. She looked over to her sister.

"It's got nothing to do with you Michelle. You're forgetting that we're are all adults here." The two got out of the car.

The twins walked to the back door their mother's. Her birds were lively and happy for the company. Michelle sat at the kitchen table going through the mail.

"Ok, fair enough. Hypothetically speaking, if Jessica comes back today your situation is an immediate shit show." Michelle said.

"If Jessica shows up today, tomorrow or next week she has a whole shit ton of explaining to do. She's pregnant by the way."

Ashley immediately regretted blurting that out. She put her hand on her forehead as she looked out the kitchen window.

"What!? How do you know that?" Michelle asked.

Ashley looked at the floor and then her sister.

"Jonas found a positive pregnancy test yesterday." "Whoa!" Michelle reacted to the news in shock.

"But wait is it; oh wow." Michelle sat back in her chair in thought. "That guy she was with. She ran off, oh whoa." She was taken back.

"Exactly." Ashley said.

"Jo told me they haven't been together since Memorial Day. I am trusting you to keep this extremely under wraps this news effects more than just Jonas it could impact your future in laws as you put it. It would be smart not to mention this to Colin."

"Ashley. That is huge news. He must hold you in high regard. Or is he just vulnerable at this point? Michelle asked.

"Enough. You are now in the know. Did you talk to Colin about that other thing?" Ashley asked.

"Did I talk to Colin? Yeah I talked to Colin some this morning. Did I talk to Colin about him having sex with Hailey Martin just before Memorial Day? No I didn't mention it."

"Michelle, it is just a rumor."

Michelle was going thru the mail. She started slamming letters down that weren't addressed to her.

"That bitch was there last night with her parents, he had his fucking arm around her."

"What did you do? You say anything to him?" Ashley brought a coffee over and sat down.

"What? Make a scene, no. I did the only thing I could do." She looked at her sister and ran her hand through her hair.

"What's that?" Ashley asked.

"Somebody made a dumb joke, I began to laugh as fake and as phony as I could. He looked at me and I just stared at him smiling. He got the hint and moved away offering wine to everyone."

"He is good at playing it off." Ashley said.

"We talked about it this morning. He started to get overly serious and apologetic. I think he thought I was going to break it off with him."

"You laid it on a little think huh?"

"Like molasses. He told me he loved me." Michelle said.

"Oh my, you don't play fair." Ashley said.

"I love him Ashley, I do. I told him so this morning and I meant it. I can look beyond Hailey. But remember what dad used to say." The twins looked at one another.

"Don't get played." The one said after the other.

Chapter 13

Jonas began packing his bag. He heard car door close it was Colin and George out front. His phone buzzed again this time it was the hospital.

"This is Dr. Parker, I am waiting on a callback from HR."

He walked out on the deck and waved to the two of them as they approached.

"Yes ma'am, yes ma'am extended sick leave that is correct. Bereavement."

Colin and George looked at to one another then to Jonas.

"Yes I understand. My father has been placed on hospice with lung and pancreatic cancer. Yes could be tomorrow could be in three weeks. Ma'am you don't have to apologize I understand the reasoning for the line of questioning."

Jonas leaned on the banister. George removed his hat and turned away. Colin looked to him and noticed he was tearing up.

"Thank you ma'am, yes this is a good number for long distance. Thanks again." He closed his phone.

"I have a flight for Des Moines this evening connecting through Philly."

Colin looked at Jonas. "I'm sorry man."

"Thank you."

Colin went to Jonas and the two friends hugged. George turned around and embraced the two of them.

"You just take as long as you need Jonas. We will be here for you. You have my word." George kept his arm around him.

"I going with you." Colin said.

"I appreciate the thought very much. This is something I need to deal with on my own."

Just then a car horn sounded. It was Mary out front George went to see her waving his arms for her to cease.

"Come in the house I have to show you something before I forget." Jonas looked twice ensuring they wouldn't be followed.

The two went through the glass slider, "follow me to the laundry." he said.

"What is it man?" Colin asked. Jonas made sure George and Mary were still out front.

"This."

I found this in the trash yesterday. He handed him the test Colin he gave it a look over. His eyes shifted and then back to Jonas. "Positive, huh. Jess, Jess." Colin said.

"It's not yours, is it?" Jonas shook his head back and forth slowly.

"She had her cycle since our last time." Jonas said.

"You talked to Ashley didn't you?" Colin asked.

He replied. "The two of them on the beach. Yeah."

"So that's what this is really all about. I am sorry I didn't say anything to you. I wanted to talk to Jess first but then everything happened to quick."

The sliding glass door had opened. "Where you men at?" George said. "They wanted you to extend your lease through the end of the year, that's why we showed up," Colin said.

Colin handed the test back to Jonas, he put it in a white envelope and then into his pocket. The two went out front.

Colin looked to his dad "We were just looking at the dryer vent. It's fine."

Jonas waved to Mary she was on the deck waiting. He went to greet her. She immediately came to him with a hug.

"Oh Jonas, I am awful sorry to hear this news." "Thank you."

"Hey, let me give you a lift to the bus station." Colin said.

"That I will take we need to go in the next hour or so." He replied.

The Sanderson's stood there on the deck with Jonas. George insisted on saying a quick prayer for Jim Parker and the safe travels of his son.

Chapter 14

The two sat in Colin's car at the bus station parking lot.

"Let me ask you something man. What kept you from proposing after the gorge?" Colin asked.

Jonas turned away and looked at family crossing the parking lot with their luggage.

"You're the only one who can answer that." Jonas looked back to Colin briefly. Then stared off again chewing his thumb nail.

"We all saw them together on the beach that day. Talk about timing mom came thru just as they were in a romantic embrace and I thought I saw them kiss."

"That's what Ashley said, Mary came thru." Jonas said.

"I am sorry. Man I should've told you about it as soon as it happened. But I needed to hear it from her first before I jump to any conclusions. She said Josh was just a work colleague."

"I know I get it man, what are you going to do not believe her?" Jonas said.

"Then shortly thereafter she has travel plans for Florida something about medical screening."

"Yeah that's accurate." Jonas said.

"Here's the kicker man, if you ask me it's almost like she was trying to get noticed with another man."

"What do you mean?" Jonas asked.

"For one walking passed my parent's house, then they were seen making out at the spot on more than one occasion. All in broad daylight."

Jonas looked to his friend. "Do you think she was trying to get back at me for not proposing?"

"I would put thoughts like that out of your mind. I got something else to tell you, not trying to overwhelm you but you should hear it from me."

"Geez man. How much more is there?" Jonas rubbed his forehead with both hands.

"Jess used her mom's landline as a backup phone number on the flight reservation. The airline called Patty's to confirm. Patty called my parents confused about the reservation Jess made. She listed Josh Michaels on the reservation."

"Listen man, I'm going to put all my cards on the table. Ok. I was too chicken shit to propose to her, ok.

Something inside of me says that this girl wants more than what I can give in life, as a partner and as a husband. Read the letter she sent me." Jonas handed it over to Colin.

"Right there man 'mistake getting back together, priorities not bonded' and on and on. We needed a break a few years ago, so we did. There was resentment building that's why she went to New York."

"Wait that's why you guys briefly broke up?" Colin said.

"Long distance relationships don't work man not in this life and certainly not in this profession. Then I was the one initiating us to get back together. After an entire year, I missed her man. I felt no good without her."

"When was the last time you talked to her?" Colin asked.

"Almost a week ago, I tried to keep the conversation light but then we end up shouting. The last time I called her was before I saw you on the beach yesterday morning, I got her voicemail."

"What prompts the shouting?"

"Colin, you have no clue how dangerous it is down there, no clue. But Jess does, and she took off anyway with Michaels."

"You said something about that yesterday at the beach. What are you telling me?"

The bus was pulling up and the two men exited the car. Colin popped the trunk.

"I'm saying people go missing down there and they're lucky to be recovered alive. She and Michaels both know that."

The two men looked at each other.

"So are you taking your letter and a used pregnancy test to Iowa? What as reminders? Or to torture yourself?" Colin asked.

"I put the stick test back where I found it originally, in the bathroom trash."

His phone began to buzz, he knew it would be Ashley. Colin perked up at the sound of it.

"Better get that it might be Ashley." Colin said smiling. Jonas looked at the phone display AW.

"Exactly right, I'm not so innocent now either."

"Bro at this point, does it really matter? Call us if you need anything." Colin said. The two fist bumped and Jonas walked to the bus.

He answered his phone.

"Hello."

"So let me guess you decided to go fishing instead of lying next to me in the sun, I see where I stand." she said in a joking manner.

"I'm sorry about that Ashley. I'm flying to Des Moines tonight, my dad is on hospice."

"What?"

Chapter 15

He was delayed in Philadelphia for much of the night and slept where and when he could. He was alert and exhausted functioning on three and half cups of coffee he was finally getting into Rockport. It's been seven and a half years he thought. Seven and a half years since he had shown his face in town January 1994. He kept in touch where he could with both Mitch and Troy. Due to the many bad memories the O'Conner's relocated themselves to Florida as a family. Mitch became a network administrator for a law firm and married a young woman in the same field of work. Stacy recovered many of her faculties thru rehab and the crutch of family. The last email he had from Mitch said that Stacy still suffers from migraines and doesn't drive due to a partial loss of vision from her left side. Otherwise she was in good spirits and had met a man in church that she had been seeing. Many old acquaintances stayed in town and worked the economy from agriculture and livestock to the cement plant along with a few rock quarries. These were the life blood business that made the town. The local hospital, police and emergency services were also good jobs for townies such as Troy Payton. Troy stayed local and worked his way up in the local banking and credit unions starting as a teller and making his way as a loan officer. Troy became the local point of contact for the many functions of the Chamber of Commerce. He was already a second degree mason. A ranking member with the Rockport JaySis, town council and rotary club. Troy knew how to network and be available to people. They all went to see Troy for loans and financing for farm equipment, automobiles and mortgages. Troy brought in a lot of business. The bank board of trustees made him the youngest vice president they ever had. Troy was engaged to Jenny Wills for a period of time, the two were also living together. Troy was insecure to say the least. He was in a prior relationship where he caught his then girlfriend Shannon Oswald in bed with an older man.

Troy's relationship trouble with Jenny began on a simple couples' night out of drinking, darts and dancing at County Bar and Grill. Jenny's sister Alison and her boyfriend liked to have a good time and put people on the spot especially Alison. Most of the time it was all in good fun and not meant to hurt feelings. Until the subject matter of 'who did you lose your virginity to' came up in drunken conversation,

"Keep your mouth shut Alison! Do not say." Jenny was very serious.

Troy sat back in his chair.

"Ya know. You are making a huge deal about this. Now I want to know. You always said it someone who I don't know and doesn't live around here anymore." Troy said then taking a swig of beer.

"I told you I wasn't going to tell and to respect my privacy." Jenny said.

"Jonas." Alison blurted out then laughed. Jenny looked at Alison in disbelief. Troy didn't say anything. He just turned to his girlfriend with a look of shock. His mouth was partially open as he comprehended what was just said. Jenny turned away in tears. This night ended very earlier. Jenny didn't speak to her sister for nearly a year after this intentional mishap.

The couple tried to move forward in the relationship but it was Troy's stubbornness that wouldn't get out of the way.

"Why would you lie to me about Jonas? Is he the one you really want to be with?"

"I lied because I knew you would react this way. It happened six years ago in high school."

This line of questioning went on twice a month for the next four months and then Troy ended the relationship.

At this point Jonas had decided that time away was best for him due to life distractions. He went away for medical school and decided not to look back for a while. Once he was setup in New England he received a letter forwarded from his dad's address. A very unfriendly letter from Troy.

Hey Captain America.

How could you not tell me that you had sex with Jenny? When I told you I was interested in her you immediately should've have told me that you had been with her. I would not have gotten serious with her, I would not have told her that I loved her over and over or bought an engagement ring.

Her sex life comes out in front of everybody at the bar and to find out that she's been lying to me about it. Why did she lie Jonas? How many times did you fuck my girlfriend?

I can't be married to a girl that one of my best friends has been with.

You cheated me.

You've always had sound judgment but if I ever see you again……. I better not see you again.

———————————————

Jonas did not return the correspondence nor did he call his now former friend. He figured that time away would make it better. Eventually.

More concerning to Jonas was his father. He missed the holidays in 1993 staying with random women he knew from truck stop to truck stop. At times he was just flat out on the road. Or worse yet laying drunk somewhere to be taken advantage of. That was the fear his mother would instill in her son that his father was living a dangerous lifestyle even though he always seemed to be doing well financially. He was tired of watching his father self-destruct. He had attempted rehab but would never take it seriously.

Unfortunately some of his old acquaintances also fell into similar pitfalls of life. Keith Bowers being the primary topic of local wasted youth. Keith graduated from Rockport Central and opted not to attend state college. But rather to work for his father who owned the County Bar in town. Keith was a success and well liked in town. Mostly due to his glory days playing football for his dad. He essentially became his father's right hand man in dealing with sponsors, vendors, dart and pool leagues. All of Keith's high school buddies who had stayed local often frequented County Bar & Grill. Eventually Keith met and fell in love with a young lady by the name of Anna Grosling who had transplanted herself to Rockport from Anaheim, California. Her parents were divorced and her father had retired from the military a few years prior. Her father Bill worked third shift at one of the rock quarries. Not many people saw Bill out in town. He was known as drinker. The police responded to Bill's once because he shot his coffee table with his .38. He told the police he accidentally dropped the gun.

Anna herself was looking for a fresh start away from her mother in California who took to living like a gypsy as she put it. Anna was 24 in 1992, Keith about to turn 23 when he met Anna. She found the bar scene and men naturally gravitated to her. She was slim and pretty with sandy brown hair. The local women townies immediately labeled Anna as the town slut. She had a habit to play men and even had two men fight over her in the bar parking lot once. Keith and Anna became exclusive in late 1993 eventually moving in together. Keith had propped Anna up on a pedestal. Some of Keith's closest friends were very happy for the two of them. Others became generally concerned for him over time.

The couple seemed to be in love. Keith's parents had been very skeptical of Anna and her motives. Whatever she wanted Keith made it happen. She could do nothing wrong in his mind. Keith spoiled her with cars and trips to Mexico and Mardi Gras.

Keith's parents noticed that their son's general attitude was becoming unpleasant when in dialogue about their relationship. His father had accused him of being high on something during working hours. His father noticed this trend more and more as the days and months passed.

The Bowers always had Sunday dinner at their house. The tradition had started when their oldest daughter had gotten married and had a family of her own. As the months went on Anna seemed not to feel well on Sundays and would not attend Sunday dinner. Many times Keith's family members voiced their concerns about Anna taking advantage of him, he would not hear of it and promptly became agitated. Keith and his father nearly came to blows when his father refused to give him a raise at the bar. Keith had setup a very profitable sports trivia night. This began a divide with his parents. Keith had stopped coming to Sunday dinner during this time.

Keeping Anna happy was Keith's top priority. His mother questioned Anna's loyalty to her son. His mother had noticed how friendly and free spirited she was. Keith's mother had heard from her peers that Anna was seen riding around town with various people women and men. Anna loved attention especially from men.

In the summer of 1995 Anna was due to have her first child. The Bowers had seemed to reconcile with her and became more accepting of Anna. There was a noticeable change in both Keith and Anna. Rumors of alcohol and drug use had gotten around town. Anna gave birth to baby boy that summer. But by years end she had decided to leave Keith for Duane Hanson. Many unconfirmed rumors circled this change but Keith took no action. He accepted the baby as his. Anna packed her and the baby and moved in with Duane.

Anna's games began from there. She would tell Keith to meet her somewhere and then never show up. She demanded money constantly for her and the baby. He would give Anna what he could. That year Keith was arrested for driving under the influence and procession of a controlled substance. Anna refused to allow him to see the baby after his arrest to include his family. These were dark days for Keith he had taken a week off to clear his mind keeping to himself. He called his older brother who lived in Cedar Valley around midnight on that Thursday and told him that he loved him and then hung up the phone. His brother called him back to no response. He then called the police and asked them to conduct a welfare check at Keith's residence. At approximately one thirty in the morning the state patrol showed up at Keith's knocking at the door. He became alarmed and frantic he couldn't make sense as to why they were there. Keith had been self-medicating and was not mentally competent. After a six hour standoff with police he came out of his house brandishing a .12 gauge shotgun allegedly. Keith was shot dead inside his fence line by the police.

Anna distanced herself. She bounced around various relationships years after Keith's death. She was found dead of drug overdose a few years later, not long after her father had passed away. Several other classmates and high school friends had been in and out of jail or doing time for petty theft, domestic violence and drug possession.

It was early dawn and Jonas was driving through the west part of town. He noticed a new high school and surrounding many new homes. Old houses were torn down and rebuilt to a modern feel. New car dealerships, restaurants and professional offices were present on both sides of the road. Looks pretty good he thought as he

made a turn toward his fathers. It was warm
and humid at dawn when pulled into the
driveway at his father's house. He always
wondered why dad never sold the house
after the divorce. It just seemed to be too
much house for a truck driver who lived at
truck stops most of the time. The old house
now had bright yellow siding, the lawn was
severely over grown. The staple of the lot
was the massive maple tree out front with
many dead leads a top. He parked, grabbed
his bag and walked to the side door of the
garage. Jonas went through his many keys
finally finding the right one. He inserted it to
find the door was unlocked. The garage was
stale and hot from the summer. Jim Parker
had every tool imaginable in his garage and
perfectly labeled. Everything looked
untouched which gave Jonas the feel at
home again. The spare house key was in an
old small coffee can on a shelf in the back.
He grabbed the set and left the garage
locking the door he entered through. He
grabbed his bag and went to the door he
used to run through, his dad still hadn't
replaced the screen door. He opened the
back door to the kitchen it was dark inside
and hot. He walked through shutting and
locking the door behind him. Jonas walked
to the front to the thermostat and turned on
the air conditioning. He tossed his bag on

the living room couch and looked around noticing familiar items. He saw an old knitted blanket his grandmother had made many years ago next to this his father's recliner. He sat in the recliner, kicked his shoes off, draped the blanket over him then reclined the chair. His shifted himself to the right and truly felt at ease, he sighed and drifted to sleep. He was home.

He suddenly awoke to the sound of an ambulance off in the distance. He sat up and reached for his cell, two missed calls from his mother no voicemail. He called her.

"Hello good morning Jonas."

"Hi, I made it."

"Oh I know we drove by your father's house twice already and saw the rental we then hit the grocery store. What are your plans honey?"

"I'm going to hit the bathroom, hit the shower and then get over to the care center. Probably stop for a coffee along the way. I also need to charge my phone. So yeah you know." he said.

"Jonas just so you know the care center has certain house rules about low noise levels for the patients there. Your father is in room 117 on the first floor. They have an attendant at the front as you go through the sliding doors you know."

"That sounds about right. Thankyou."

"Would you like to go the mall after and visit? We should really discuss a few things."

"Mom unless you and Rick have something planned I want to keep this afternoon open to dad."

The phone was silent Jonas could here muffled discussion in the background.

"You're right honey I'm sorry. Go visit and be with your dad and maybe call me after we would love to have you for dinner, or something. Ok, love you."

"You, too." he said and closed his phone.

He got up and went to his bag. He gathered his shaving kit and phone charger. He went to the bathroom and got the shower going then charged his phone in the kitchen. He walked to the front of the house and opened the front door stepping out on the enclosed porch and took in the humidity. He listened to the sound of where he had grown up. Neighborhood looks the same he thought. He went back in closing and locking the door behind and hit the shower.

He was not looking forward to conversing about big ticket items with his mother. The years after his parent's divorce were tough. His father had a bad habit of saying terrible things about his former wife and Jonas would have to listen to it all. The same thing would happen when he stayed with his mother. Sara was more incessant about everything especially his affairs with Kathy Wilder and that ruined relationship. Even though Sara had moved on in life with Rick McCarthy she was still bitter. His life distractions were not limited to one parent.

Thinking about those times retrospectively he remembered Rick rolling his eyes in the distance during one of his mother's rants. Growing up with two bitter parents was tough. Jonas immersed himself in school and sports to avoid the noise from his parents. The only times his parents were seen in public were at their sons sporting events. They agreed to always be civil for those moments.

He drove over to the nursing care center and began to dread what his mother

143

wanted to talk him about. Clearly he has a last will and testament. But what does she want the house? He thought.

He took notice how the various business parks were immaculately groomed and landscaped. He drove the parking lot, parked and walked to the entry of the sliding doors. The attendant greeted him.

"Sir"

"Hi. I think my dad is in room 117."

"Mr. Parker, yes he's awake the nurses just did shift change. You can go visit it's the second to the last door on the right."

He look down the deep hallway. He took a deep breath and thought how difficult this was going to be. He began walking taking his time. He could see the entry to his father's room as a nurse exited walking towards him. She took four or five steps and the two made eye contract.

"Oh wow Jenny Wills. How is he?" Jonas motioned to his father.

She stopped and put her hand over her mouth and took a moment to look him over. "Oh Jonas, oh my. You are missed terribly." The two hugged.

She pulled away nodding her head forward looking to his father's room.

"Jim has had his meds and is resting comfortably. I am on shift you can buzz if you need something. I have rounds. I'll be back through soon. Hey, welcome back." He smiled and waved to her as she went to another room.

He entered the room and his father turned over to recognize him. He smiled. His father looked forty pounds lighter and very frail from the last time he saw him.

"Well then I assume your mother phoned you?" His father whispered.

"Yeah."

His father was weak.

"Sport let me look at you."

He took a chair close to his father's bed.

The two smiled at each other. He took his father's hand. His father coughed suddenly the sound was awful.

"Dr. Parker. My son the doctor." he said quietly.

"Yeah how about that huh." Jonas felt both awkward and sad at the sight of his father. What do you say to your father on his death bed he thought.

"You done me proud son." He began to tear up. Jonas too. He squeezed his father's hand.

"You stayin at the house, right?"
"Yes Sir."

"Take what you want back with you, you mother is just going to throw out what she can't sell anyway."

"I don't understand?" Jonas said.

"I had to make some snap decisions and gave your mother power of attorney."

Jonas pressed his lips together and nodded his head.

"This diagnosis came on quick, fucking cancer anyway. They found a buyer for my two trucks, trailers and what not."

"What does 'what not' mean dad?" He asked quietly. His dad turned away.

"I had to sell my house too." His father became emotional. He tried to calm him.

"Just take it easy dad you have a lot of tubes in you, it's just a house."

He turned back to his son. "When you watch your own child grow up year after year and eventually leave for good it's more than just a house, it's a lifetime."

Jonas bowed his head and began to sob.

"I did everything wrong. The hard way, and it cost me my marriage and some good living. I did some stupid things."

"Dad I don't hear anybody complaining." He looked up.

"As you age you become your biggest critic. You'll see, every man has to look at himself in the mirror. Depending on the man, the mirror can run pretty deep." His dad sighed and coughed dreadfully.

"Pull that string for the nurse I am feeling a pain in my side." Jonas did as his father asked. Within moments a young nurse and Jenny walked in. Jonas stood up and got out of the way toward the entry of the room. Jenny stood next to him as she supervised the attending nurse.

"Mr. Parker, were here." The young nurse said.

147

"Are you expecting someone?" Jenny asked him.

"Maybe my mother, why?" "No silly I know Sara. There is a very tan nice looking young woman who asked for you out front." He looked to Jenny strangely. "Thank you." he said.

He walked very quickly to the attendant area. Can't be he thought. There she was enjoying the lobby aquarium.

"Ashley."

"Hey." She stood up and came over to him.

"You're a wonderful sight." He was suddenly filled with a shot of life and joy at the sight of her.

"You've been crying, is there anything I can do?" She kissed him and then hugged him.

"Jonas." A voice called out.

He waved to Jenny. He put his arm around Ashley and walked over.

"Ashley is my friend Jenny Wills." "Hi. Jenny Hogan nowadays you've been gone awhile." She smiled. Jonas looked at Ashley, "Jenny this is my girlfriend Ashley

Winters." Ashley looked a Jonas and smiled. The two ladies shook hands.

"Your dad is out like a light, probably for the next hour or two. If you have any errands now would be a good time. Good to meet you." she said.

"Nice to meet you." Ashley replied.

"Here take my cell phone number in case any, you know." he said.

"Leave it with front desk they will call you." she said in a quiet voice.

"Thank you for taking care of him." They waved as Jenny walked away. He and Ashley exited he held her close to his side. He look at her and was happy.

"So to what do I owe this surprise?" He asked.

"I lost my dad last year and I can't let someone I care about go through this alone." she said pressing herself into him.

Chapter 16

Mid-day in Iowa was hot and humid. He was cleaning the intake of the lawn mower. Ashley took a shower and was taking a nap, tired from travel. His mother had pulled up to the house and approached him.

"Doing chores?" she said.

"The lawn takes twenty five minutes you know that."

"I see another rental car."

"My girlfriend Ashley. She's asleep right now."

"Can we take a walk around the block like we used to?" His mother asked.

He tossed his rag to the ground and went with his mother.

"So how did it go?" She asked.

"Hard to take, but we communicated. Dad said you had power of attorney."

"Yes. We have a buyer for his assets and that essentially takes care of his affairs. He owns everything out right. We just need to pay the hospice which we have prorated with Renee."

"Mom. Thank you, thank you. I would be up a creek without a paddle without you in this." "It's the least I could do." she said.

They turned the corner and stopped at the city park swing sets. The birds were chirped at their arrival. He could tell his mother was nervous.

"Jonas it's been a long time since I've seen you. Sometimes, I uh. I don't know how to talk to you because I think you hate me." His mother stood there her jaw quivered.

"I'm sorry honey. I'm so sorry for everything you saw, everything you heard and every negative family thought you had until you left. I think about how inappropriate I was with my conduct back then. I saw you with your father in his truck that morning. There are no words to right that wrong. I was vindictive, I had no right. I was very toxic at times. I had no right to trash my former husband in front of our son. I said some awful, awful things Jonas that I can't undo. For years your mother was a black hole."

Her voice began to crack. "And I know you hate me for it." He tried to stop her in midsentence. "I don't hate you." He took her by the hand and kissed it. She cleared her throat and reached into her bag.

"Well I hope not I am you mother."

"There is one last piece of business. If you want to have it signed over to you or not no pressure from us."

"What's that?" He asked.

She handed him three keys. He looked her curiously. "The cabin." he said.

"We would love to have you back in our lives." She stood firm and looked her son eye to eye and began to cry. "The thought of a grandchild fishing there with my son never crossed my mind."

"Mom." He began to cry and embraced her. She was his mother and he loved her.

They walked back to the house together laughing and crying. He felt good. He saw Rick had parked behind his mother and was on the side walk as they approached.

"Hey Rick."

"Hi Jonas welcome home bud. I uh, came over after they called."

"The care center?" Jonas said.

Sara looked at Rick.

"I think they tried you." Rick said.

Jonas didn't say another word. He immediately jumped into his rental and drove to the care center. He cursed himself for not taking his cell phone with him when walking with his mother. Later in life he described leaving them and driving like he was traveling thru time. He ran a stop sign entering the parking lot. He shut the car off and ran through the doors and saw Jenny standing outside his father's room.

"I'm sorry Jonas." She was crying and they hugged one another.

He walked in the room and sat in the chair he took earlier. He sat with his father holding his hand for over an hour. The cancer had made his father a frail and weak man. He heard someone enter from behind keeping his eyes on his father. Ashley came behind him and wrapped her arms around him.

"Hi Ashley."

"Hey. I love you." she said quietly.

"I love you too. This is my father Jim."

Chapter 17

He stood in the back of the funeral home with his mother and Ashley as many people lined up to recognize the family of Jim Parker. It was a sad day. Many pictures of Jim and his son in pop warner football were on display. Jim pitching to Jonas. Many others with the three of them as a family. Rick made a point to stay out front and organize with the funeral people. The forecast called for rain he helped erect a sidewalk canopy out front and directed parking. Coach Bowers was making his way through with his signature crew cut.

"Hi Sara, damn sorry to hear about this." he said. She smiled and nodded.

"Thankyou."

"We certainly miss you around here Jonas. I'm sorry about your dad. We all liked him." He hugged Jonas.

"Keith would've been happy to see you back in town." He started to step away.

"Coach I was terribly hurt when I heard the news about Keith. I was in school I couldn't make it back."

"I know son, we understand fully." He stepped towards Ashley.

"This is my girlfriend Ashley."

"Hello." she said.

"This is your guy, huh." He pointed to Jonas.

"Yes, yes he is." She smiled.

"Well young lady you got a good one. I am sorry for your loss." "Thankyou."

Mrs. Bowers followed her husband very broken up. She hugged Sara and kissed both Jonas and Ashley. Her husband led her to her seat. Ashley looked to Jonas.

Troy Payton suddenly appeared and gave Sara hug. "It's good to see you again Troy." Sara glanced over at her son.

He was followed by a young woman that he introduced as his wife. It suddenly began to rain and many people looked out the windows.

"Jo, sorry for your dad man." Jonas nodded and smiled at them. "Thankyou." There was a sudden crack of thunder and flash of lightning.

"This is my wife Kelly." "Pleasure to meet you, this my girlfriend Ashley." The four shook hands. They walked on to their seats. It rained hard that day.

Chapter 18

The month of August had come and gone. The two had spent many hours and days going through the house in Rockport and selling off what they could with the help of Sara and Rick. His father's house was now empty and pending sale. Jonas had set aside the small items of sentimental value he was bringing back with him at the cabin. He was staying at the cabin finishing his town and tax affairs for the cabin. Ashley had left to go back to work and then returned to help him with the cabin. She was due to leave for good in the afternoon. In the morning they took a small boat out to a sandbar in the river.

"Yes, woo-hoo! That's is two big cats in ten minutes Jonas my boy." Ashley said with excitement reeling in another catfish.

"It's the same fish. Two twenty inchers in less than ten minutes come on?" he said.

"You're just jealous of me, hey I'm for hire if you need someone to catch fish for you." she said laughing.

"Ok, that was over the top." He watched her unhook the fish and toss it back. She handled herself well on the river.

"Hey, hey here I go. Gotcha." He reeled in a nice fish half the size of hers.

"You know I haven't been out here since dad caught mom with Rick that morning." He tossed the fish.

"Really." She casted into the river.

"Then three weeks ago she handed me the keys after we shared a moment together." he said.

"Ok. Where you going with this?" She took two steps back in the muck and began to reel the line in looking at him.

"I feel like a phony. Almost like I'm dishonoring dad. After everything happened he stopped bringing me here. My grandfather built the cabin it was a source of dad's heritage. I missed this place through high school and college."

"It still is a part of his and your heritage. Is that why it took over two weeks for you to come down here?" She asked.

"I'm not sure. She gave me the keys and I feel a dark cloud over this place."

"Like she's passing off this baggage to you now?"

"Yeah in an odd way, and I am supposed to make something good come out of it."

"She apologized to you, right? Your dad trusted her with power of attorney."

"I know all that. That doesn't mean I don't still have emotions to the height of their breakup."

"I get it. You can be hard to read sometimes especially these last few weeks." she said tossing the line.

"To be honest with you I don't feel like I am even from here anymore. At the wake I barely felt like I have anything remotely in common with anyone. I'm just this distant person who used live here. I can't talk to Troy." He continued to cast and reel in his line.

"Jonas. How would you react if you found out abruptly and in front of people that I had sex with Colin a few years before us? You wouldn't react well especially if I lied to you about it. You would feel betrayed."

His mind wondered to the affair between Jessica and Josh. He didn't understand Troy's position from the letter he received. He had himself convinced of a distorted reality at the time he thought. He kept the letter with the bank return address. He thought of replying.

"Jonas? Are you listening to me?"

"Yes, you're probably right he feels betrayed and Jenny should have been upfront." "Exactly."

"We should probably get going for Des Moines." His mind was a stir.

Chapter 19

An airline announcement amplified, "Now boarding the remaining rows."

She stood up and gathered her belongings.

"Shit my phone is going to die. Damnit." She and Jonas held another.

"So, when am I going to see you back on the east coast?" She asked.

"End of the week, I'll be back."

"Promise?" "Yeah, pending anything crazy. I have to get my name on the deed then button up the cabin and take mom and Rick out for dinner maybe. I have all my stuff packed. I've been practically living out of my shaving kit last two days."

"Final boarding all remaining rows ladies and gentlemen all remaining rows." "Better go." The two took in one another. "I love you Jo." "I love you too." She stepped away to the airline agent. She turned back and waved. He winked. They both were smiling.

———————————————————

He pulled into the cabin driveway and went inside. He walked through thinking he didn't have much to do from what he told Ashley. He went and grabbed a beer from the fridge along with a pen and notebook. He began to write.

Troy.

Thank you for attending Dad's wake. He really enjoyed you and Mitch. Especially watching us on the field. My parents always kept things civil during football and baseball season.

On June 1st 1987 I lost my virginity to Jenny at her Cedar Street house. She made me promise not to tell anyone. I kept my word.

We were kids Troy.

We were still kids when you wrote seven years ago.

You put a lot on my plate with your letter.

Should have I told you about it once you expressed your interest for her? I don't know. How would you have felt if I did?

I was in college and not around but for summer. Jenny should've told you. She requested me not to tell anyone.

Troy It only happened the one time. And you let a lifetime end up with Mike Hogan over a mind full of insecurity. – Jo

His letter was never sent. It remained in the cabin.

It was Labor Day in the middle of the night. His woke suddenly to his cell phone buzzing. It must be Ashley calling he thought to himself. He grabbed his phone from the night stand.

"Sanderson?" he said aloud.

"Hello?"

"Jonas, Jo?" "Yeah Colin."

"Dude you need to get back here right now!" He pulled the phone away from the shouting of the ear piece.

He could hear chatting in the background.

"Colin calm down man what is going on?" He was still half asleep.

"We got word this evening that Josh Michaels is dead and Jessica is missing, they believe kidnapped."

He went numb and couldn't think clearly from the shocking words. He must not have heard that correctly.

164

"What?!"

"Josh Michaels is dead! Murdered! Dude that's not all there is a package for you here Patty brought up from Mass. It's addressed to you with Jessica's parents address."

"That makes no sense. What kind of package?"

"It's a yellow envelope, feels kinda like video tape inside. Jonas there are federal agents at my parent's house." Colin said loudly.

"I'm on my way."

Chapter 20

Back at the airport he was getting coffee at a kiosk. He checked his phone two missed calls from Ashley and one from Colin. He shook his head. He didn't want to tell his mother the details of his departure. He couldn't believe what Colin told him over the phone. How could this happen he thought.

"I just don't understand leaving so suddenly like this. You were already booked for the end of the week." Sara said.

Rick looked away and rolled his eyes. "Sara he is grown man for Pete's sake."

He turned and faced his mother. They smiled at one another.

"Mom I've been here a month. I need to get back to my life. The cabin is locked up and I need go. I love you."

Announcement coming. "Remaining five rows boarding."

She grabbed her son and embraced him hard. "I love you too. I am so proud of my boy the doctor." She began to cry. "You call me ok, soon."

166

He looked at Rick. "See you soon Rick, give my best to Renee." "I'll do that, you travel safe now and try to come home for Christmas." The two embraced. He promptly walked to the agent at the gate and called Ashley as he hit the jet way. No answer straight to voicemail.

'This is Ashley Winters with' he pressed one to leave a message.

"Hey I'm coming home. Is there any chance of picking me up at the bus station say six forty five? Love you." He shut the phone off.

He buckled his seat belt and watched the steward staff conduct the aircraft safety brief. As the plane broke away and turned he could see mom and Rick through the windows. She pointed to her son as she blew him kisses. He waved and acknowledged her. He put his head back and closed his eyes. He was worried and scared for Jessica.

He dreamed of being on the hospital ship playing cards with the engine room mechanics and winning a hand and laughing as they slammed their cards down. He dreamed of walking the port-o side walk and talking to the bar tender girl about her brother's leg that he treated. She kissed him

167

suddenly as she was grateful to him. He then dreamed of Ashley and Michelle laughing and pointing to him from the beach asking to go fishing. He walked to them on the beach but they disappeared. Like they were never there. He dreamed of himself at one of the popular discotheques that everyone tried to frequent. There were many people around crowded. Miss Y walked passed him wearing medical scrubs her head was bloodied. Blood was stained on her scrubs. She pointed at him and then walked away. All he could do was stare awkwardly at her. He dreamed of talking to the Captain on the bridge of the ship. He couldn't understand what he was saying. Slow motion he turned around and went below decks to the hospital. He passed Josh Michaels at the pharmacy. "Where's Jessica?" Michaels shrugged his shoulders and disappeared. He saw some business girls in the ship's hospital as he found himself tied to chair with all the medical personnel around him working as if he wasn't there. There was a large mirror in front of him with someone looking through a microscope. It was Jessica she raised her heard and turned to him saying something he couldn't understand. He looked into the mirror where Rico Ortiz appeared with a gun to his head, 'NO'!!!

Chapter 21

The plane landed and shook the passengers violently as it slowed and slowed breaking hard. "Sorry for the hard landing folks", "Ladies and gentlemen welcome to Boston where the local time is five thirty three and seventy five degrees." He woke up fully as passengers were exiting the airplane. He turned his phone on buzzing with a message.

"Ashley here. Six forty five got it. Heads up the Sanderson house is high drama and Michelle overheard them asking about you." This is some bad shit he thought to himself exiting the plane through the jet way. I need to find the bus. He took two steps into the terminal as two men approached him "Dr. Parker" the taller man said with a noticeable Latino accent. Two state troopers stood behind them. The men were dressed like were in the secret service.

"Yes, and you are?" Jonas replied. "Some identification please." The agent said. He gathered his driver's license the man went to grab it from him. Jonas held it tight.

"I asked you question." The man starred at Jonas he starred back. He let go of his id and the man nearly dropped it. He checked his id. One of the troopers stepped forward. "That's not necessary trooper."

"I'm Agent Salas with the state department. This is Agent Cabrera." The two offered a good faith hand shake and Jonas accepted. He handed Jonas his id back.

"Dr. Parker first let me apologize. We were in a time crunch and I am personally sorry that we didn't get a chance to call you prior to showing up unannounced in this fashion. We certainly don't make it a habit to drop in on people at airports like this."

"Unless were making arrests." Cabrera added. Salas looked at him.

"I understand sir, I understand. The news is very shocking to me. I am still processing it." Jonas said.

The five began walking towards the escalators. Jonas had drawn a few hard looks from travelers.

"I have a file I would like you to see, maybe fill in a few blanks regarding the Port-o." Jonas nodded his head.

"How did you know I was on this plane?" The agents looked at one another not answering. Jonas rolled his eyes.

"Ok then. You can at least tell me which office you're stationed out of and how you came across that I've been to the Port-o?"

"San Juan Sir." Cabrera said.

"We would like you to come with us. We will give you a police escort and make it much quicker ride than the bus or other transport."

"I'm not going anywhere with you until you tell me the status of Jessica Adams or what the hell happened to them." The agents looked each other.

"We are unsure at present time her status. The backstory is Ms. Adams and Mr. Michaels went by small boat to a separate island to conduct some vaccinations at an orphanage. They didn't return and neither did their boat operator. The consulate was contacted by a member of a cartel."

They continued on toward the baggage claim. The troopers were noticeably on high alert.

"We need you to help us with some information, if you are willing to cooperate." Cabrera said. He had a habit or reiterating Salas.

"I am willing to do whatever it takes to get her back safe and alive." he said.

"I need to know a few things before you exit the airport." The troopers stopped at the escalator. The three men were making their way down the escalators. Jonas put his sunglasses on. Two more troopers were waiting for them at the bottom.

"What's that?" Jonas said.

"Did you tell anyone in Iowa about your phone call with Mr. Sanderson early this morning?"

"No, why? Why do you ask?" Jonas said. He was taken by that question.

Salas did not appreciate his tone. He got himself face to face with Jonas in the baggage claim.

"Doctor I think you can appreciate the sensitivity of this matter as we make sure our options aren't compromised."

"What's that supposed to mean?" Jonas shrugged.

The doors opened to the outside. "Wait my bag." "We got you bag in the cruiser. Come now." Cabrera said.

"You arrived at the Des Moines airport with two other people this morning, who are they?" Salas asked.

Jonas could not believe what he had just heard. "How the hell do you know that?"

The two agents stood in front of the state department vehicle. They didn't answer him. There were many state troopers present. People entering and exiting the airport were starring and taking notice of the presence of law enforcement.

"My mom and her boyfriend, I told them I had to get back and that's it, they don't know anything."

He stepped back and looked oddly at both Salas and Cabrera.

"Wait a minute, just wait. You think I told the media?"

"Did you?" Agent Salas pointed his finger at him. "It is not uncommon for people to sell information like this."

"No absolutely not, here take my phone as proof."

"That won't be necessary at this time. Please get in the van."

Agent Salas sat in the front seat, Cabrera sat behind Jonas in the back. He thought of the odd déjà vu five years prior.

The trooper escort headed out from the airport for the turnpike. Driving away it began to rain.

"I have some photos to show you. The first one is graphic I am sorry for the record can you identify this man?" He handed the photo to Jonas.

He looked at the gruesome photo and turned away immediately. The agents looked at him. He gathered himself and took a deeper look. It was Josh Michaels with a hole in the back of his head. His face was partially shown from the side.

"That's Dr. Josh Michaels; of New York." He handed the photo back to the agent. Salas had a yellow file folder full of photos and notes.

"Doctor I mentioned the Port-o before. It was brought to our attention that you were kidnapped in the late spring of 1996."

"You found that out from that crooked fucking consulate didn't you? That's how the cartel is able to identify aide-workers."

Neither agent answered.

"Yes, for about thirty six hours. Then I was rescued by hired policia. At least that's what I was told." Jonas said.

"I shouldn't be discussing this as you are not immediate family. But I am willing to make an exception because of the video tape. It is addressed to you on the package envelope. Do you know why the cartel would do that?" Jonas nodded.

"During my time with the cartel Rico made subtle comments about seeing Jessica and I out in the port-o together. He implied that if didn't receive the full ransom for me that he had ideas for her. They probably think we're still together." Do you think Jessica is there?" Jonas said.

"Unsure. So you and Ms. Adams are no longer an item?" Cabrera said from the back seat. Jonas shook his head he didn't want to discuss the finer details.

"Out of privacy to the situation, she left with Dr. Josh Michaels on this mission. They do have a history together. Ok. This is the last I am speaking to you about any relationships or former relationships."

Jonas looked back at Cabrera and then to Salas in the front.

"I have more photos for you if you could identify the person and or surroundings." Salas leaned back handing the photo off.

He looked at the photo of someone asleep or half dead duct taped on a couch severely beaten. He looked at both agents and briefly laughed.

"Are you jerking my chain man?" Jonas looked at Salas then Cabrera.

"What do you mean?" "That's me in the photo." Salas grabbed the photo from Jonas in disbelief. "No that's not you." Salas shook his head.

"One hundred percent. Do you see this heavy stub wedged in the cushion next to me?" "Yes, yes. What is that?" Cabrera leaned over the seat with interest.

"It's a knife one of kidnappers left behind." "Oh, I wouldn't have guessed that." "Me neither." Cabrera said.

"Do you remember where this place is by chance?" Salas asked.

"About ten minutes up the roadway from the waterfront piers, it was a discotheque down below with apartments above. Some are modified and used for a brothel. There are many bars and discotheques in the same area with the same setup."

Jonas checked the windows traffic was heavy and it was raining with authority.

"Why did they kill Michaels? There in the ransom business aren't they?" Jonas asked.

"We believe he was executed in part to drive the price up on Ms. Adams." Cabrera said from the back seat. Jonas shook his head, "People are sick, my god Jessica."

"A few more photos." Jonas had a very good idea of the next one. He was expecting the mug shot of the dark skinned man. The man with the many aliases.

"Oh my." he said aloud. It was a mug shot of a very attractive West Indies

177

woman. The second photo was her corpse in the hallway.

"Her name to me is Ms. Y." Salas wrote that down in his pad.

"Ms. Y?" Cabrera asked. "Last one." Salas handed another photo.

It was the mug shot he was expecting that the chief had shown him from years earlier. But with no names written below.

"That's him Rico like I said before. He is alpha of the cartel he beat the hell out of me. The girl Ms. Y referred to him as Mr. X. But the policia that rescued me had numerous names for him."

"I am a little surprised that you guys don't already know who these people are. The chief of the policia that rescued me told me that his name was Rico Ortiz. He is or was a rogue pirate from Cuba." he said.

"Dr. Parker this information comes at a high price with people who are in the know or just lie for the money. You experienced this first hand. Your validation is needed. We believe the woman Ms. Y was his wife or girlfriend of Jose Rico Ortiz.

We are also certain that you are the only hostage to survive an encounter with him on an unpaid ransom. The ransom demand for Ms. Adams is over one million dollars. Now about the video tape with you name on it...."

Chapter 22

It was the ninth day of September. Rumors on the island had begun to stir with the amount of law enforcement that was back and forth from Beach Plum avenue. He had given the authorities permission to view the video tape in hopes of pinpointing Jessica's location. Nobody expected it to take as long as it was taking, stress was at high levels. The Sanderson's were the primary source of the ransom demands. Jessica's parents had been separated for the last year and were unapproachable this week unless you were with the federal government. Jonas and Ashley stood out back at George and Mary's with Colin and Michelle waiting on a call to view the video tape.

"Are you ok?" She asked.

"No. I'm not ok. I just spilled my guts to Colin's family about the most terrifying experience of my lifetime. Just to explain why my name is on the envelope. The good news is Roger, Patty & Mary stopped giving me their death looks."

Colin approached Jonas.

"Dude, I had no clue of your ordeal and you gave me every hint before you left for Iowa. You telling your story to everyone like that took ridiculous amounts of courage. I just can't believe it."

"Oh, Jonas." Michelle hugged him. "How awful."

"How did Patty find out she was pregnant?" Ashley said.

Colin's voice became elevated, "It was the mission administrators overstepping their bounds, talk about making matters worse."//

Jonas began pacing around the back walkway. He could hear the ocean's crashing waves.

"I didn't expect to relive this, not like this. I don't understand why it is taking so long and why that it is important that I watch the video." Jonas said.

"Well the intent by addressing it to you implies that someone wants you to see something. They probably have their people analyzing the video and images to make sure it's real." she said. He stopped and looked at Ashley.

"How do you know that?" Jonas asked. "I work at a law firm remember. We hire audio and video people all the time to break down evidence against clients." she said.

George stepped out back. "Ok, there ready for us." The group filed in the house. The sounds of Patty sobbing we're tough to take. George put his hand on Colin's chest as the three walked passed him.

"Jonas if I came across like an ass this week, I uh, I had no clue of what you went through. I'm sorry son." George had tears in his eyes he put his arm around him.

"You have nothing to apologize for, it been a hell of a week." They proceeded out front to the driveway.

Jonas stopped next to Colin. "I'm not ready for this." Colin said.

"We're in this together. Ok? Michelle said as she held his hand.

"Ok folks I must warn you that this video is hard to take. Dr. Parker we need to know if you recognize anything in particular."

He hit play from the blue television screen.

The video began of the floor and someone's boots. The camera was sharply brought head high and Jessica Adams sitting on her knees on a bed. Her hands and feet were restrained behind her she was just wearing her undergarments. Someone was speaking in half Latin and a hint of Portuguese in the background. A person wearing a mask went over to Jessica and ripped the tape from her mouth, she was breathing heavily and crying.

"Oh, my god." Both Michelle and Ashley said aloud. Michelle with her hand over her mouth. Jonas put his arm around Ashley. Mary briefly glared at him.

She said four words. "Jonas help me, please." The video camera was then sharply directed to the floor as a familiar voice began to speak.

"Gringo." Jonas felt a sudden bone chill from the hard accent. Everyone looked to Jonas.

"Gringo, do you know who this is? Ah yes, you know who this is. I am a nemesis to many, you couldn't forget me in this life. Gringo I have asked for high dollar for this pretty little pussy of yours. (a long pause) Gringo I have a confession to make. I do not like murdering women. (a gun shot went off and a woman screamed) It makes me feel pathetic and weak. So gringo you have until mid-day on the twelfth to comply with ransom in person. I am sure you will feel back at home in the port-o. Gringo you will go to the spot where we took you down that day, you will go alone. Gringo take or leave it, trust me you don't want her fate in my hands." The camera sharply point head high to a reflection of Rico in the mirror and then ended. He looked as sinister as ever.

The family was stunned and in shock by what they just viewed. Colin and George looked immediately to Jonas. They both had the look of fear. Mary led Patty back into the house as she sobbed.

She screamed at Jonas and the agents, "You get my baby back, please get my baby back!" Mary held her.

184

Roger stepped towards the van his anger directed at both Cabrera and Salas.

"I want know what you sons of bitches are doing to get my daughter back safe! She looks like she's been raped a dozen or so times! I want my daughter back god damn it!" George grabbed him.

"Easy Roger go easy." Roger put his hands over his face and began to sob uncontrollably.

Cabrera and Salas looked to everyone. "Mr. Adams were doing everything we can."

Roger wiped his face. "Why are we not doing this from San Juan, or somewhere closer to where my daughter is?"

"We cannot compromise information and security to this matter. It is possible that the kidnapper has people affiliated to our office on his payroll. Trust me sir. The less people the better."

Jonas looked to the agents.

"That's Rico. Back up the video to the last ten seconds or so." Jonas said suddenly. They replayed the video. "Everyone quiet everyone quiet. Turn up the volume to max."

"Do you hear that?" Jonas said to the agents. Everyone was still quite listening to the tape.

"That faint beeping noise?" Salas said. He got in the back of the van and replayed the video again. "What is that noise?" Salas asked.

"That's the crane from the water front in the port-o." Jonas said. "It sounds just like that when it changes direction. I know where she is." he said with certainty.

"You can barely hear it, how can you be so sure?" Cabrera asked.

In all the medical ports in the Indies that is the only one with an industrial crane that sounds like that. "We have to go after her." he said.

Ashley became upset and began to walk away towards her car. The agents looked at Jonas and nodded their heads.

"Thank you we were hoping you would say that." Salas said as he shook his hand. Cabrera turned to Jonas, "Alright my man let's do this." "Excuse me." Jonas said.

"Ashley, Ash wait, please." He ran the driveway after her.

She turned around suddenly and hit him in his chest with both fists as she cried. "You better tell me you're not going. How can you do this?"

"Ashley, if I don't go he is going to kill her." He held her by the shoulders looking directly at her.

"Jonas you don't know that and what if someone sees you, and you end up kidnapped again?"

"I have to go. I have to."

"No you don't." She hugged and kissed him hard as if he was already gone. They walked back together and Ashley went into the house. Jonas stayed back with the agents. Cabrera turned to Jonas.

"The ransom money is in account pending state department review. They are pretty quick on this stuff. We can get you an emergency passport in Miami. To save time we are traveling using the military trade port base in New Hampshire. Bring your driver's license and back a light bag for changing. The time is now if you are going to say good bye to your loved ones. We will be waiting."

He walked in the house. Everyone was gathered and comforting one another in the kitchen. Nobody was prepared to see Jessica in that condition. Jonas had everyone's attention. He stood at the entry of the kitchen with his arms folded to an eerie quiet. Mary held Patty and starred hard at Jonas.

Jonas approached them, "I'm not sure what to say at this point. I know deep in my soul that I have an obligation to help. Otherwise I am not sure if I can live with myself. I'm going with them."

Ashley and Michelle were crying.

"God speed son." George went to Jonas and embraced him. Colin and Michelle followed suit. Emotions were high. "I love you all." "We love you." He broke away from them and headed for the door, Ashley followed him out.

"I will be back I promise you." "I love you." Ashley said. "I love you." Mary watched from the window.

Chapter 23

Jonas had gone into the house to say goodbye.

Cabrera motioned to Salas. "So after all the interviews we've done and information collected what do you think? The real back story I mean?"

"Honestly. That she was really more in love with Dr. Michaels. The two knew that they had conceived a child in secret or maybe he didn't know. They decided to go off together on this mission. She prefers the missionary life from what the family has attested." Salas said.

"If she was really in love Josh Michaels why is she playing go fish with Mr. Iowa in there, that's what I don't understand from the letter she left him. Does she want both men?" Cabrera said shaking his head.

"Come on Carlo we've seen this before." Cabrera looked at him oddly.

"The two naval officers and the NSA case officer. She was clearly playing the two men." Salas walked to the front of the van and turned around with his arms folded.

"I think this girl is as good as dead." he said looking at the driveway asphalt.

"How can you be so sure? Rico let the girl from Aruba go for ransom." Cabrera said.

"Yeah I know that. But now he has the chance to avenge the death of his girlfriend or at least he thinks he is, some sick shit. At least the doc is manning upon the ransom, I don't know how I would've been able to convince to go to the Port-o again." Salas said.

"Yeah, what is you plan for him down there? You know there are a slew of those clubs with brothels." Cabrera asked.

"He remembers the area he was in, we'll go from there. Besides once Rico gets word that the doc is down there he'll get sloppy and come out during the daytime."

"What you want to use the doc as bait?" Cabrera said in surprise.

"I didn't say that damnit. But I have no intention of arresting Rico, read between the lines." Salas said.

The two agents watched the goodbye between Jonas and Ashley. He approached the agents.

"Ok doc. We are in another time crunch on this. We will take you over to your place and pack a quick bag and make sure you have a valid id." Jonas walked to the front of the van.

"There is something else we need to be clear on. This is something I cannot tell Jessica's family. You will probably understand this more than anyone else. Rico is a very erratic and neurotic son of a bitch. This could end badly."

"I understand." Jonas got in the van. His thoughts were on Jessica and her family his heart with Ashley.

Chapter 24

It was in the later evening hours George and Mary were in their bedroom trying to get settled for the night.

"I don't care what you say George, he should've gone with her in the first place." He laughed and shook his head.

"That's Patty talking right there, she doesn't understand why her daughter had taken up with another man." George was upset at his wife's comment.

"You will lower your voice George Sanderson. We have guests in this house." she said. George walk in front of the bed.

"The man comes to our home early after burying his father. He did so because our son imposed guilt into him. He changes his flight arrangements and then he is confronted by federal agents at the airport. He takes it all in stride and cooperates fully. Then to clear up confusion of a package, he tells everyone about the most terrifying event in his life, where it took the police killing people to save him. Not to mention that our niece has essentially tossed him aside for another man. Now Mary it's up to you can give the boy a break, huh?"

"Ok. What about the baby George? Do you really believe that he found out after she left? Mary was reading in bed and put her book down. "Your sister still thinks their together. Oh, and not to mention how convenient it is that he has moved on so quickly with another woman." Mary was being snide.

George made his way to his closet.

"I love you, but you're making a mockery out of a bad situation. Jessica knew the risks of going Mary, that's why Jonas didn't go. I don't see how you can't accept that given what the boy went through." He dropped his arms to his sides.

"The feds are due to call Roger at nine tomorrow morning, I can't do anymore of this tonight."

Chapter 25

It was a sunny Tuesday morning but the weather delayed them for over a day and hours were getting critical. They needed to be close to the Port-o and not stuck in Miami. Jonas found out there is nothing worse than waiting. Both agents were constantly on their cell phones. They had old surveillance photos of the waterfront area he was going over. He began to think of old memories on the ship. He thought of Jessica and how glad he was to see her after surviving his capture and rescue. He couldn't believe of the situation that had taken place. How could she not take the known threats serious he thought. The agents seemed to be in serious conversation in the hangar. They waved and called for Jonas to come to the front of the hangar many of the people working. Random trades' people and staff were gathering toward the front of the hangar towards the cafeteria. A comment was made from someone passing by.

"I heard on the radio there was an incident about fifteen minutes ago in New York involving an aircraft." Many people were moving forward. Jonas passed an office with a television that showed a panned out scene of Manhattan. One of the buildings from the world trade center was on fire and black thick smoke was rolling out from the top. He left the office and headed for the cafeteria where there was a bigger television. Random people started to comment and shout.

"Holy shit what the hell is that?"

"It's another plane"

"No, NO, NO, Oh My God!" Many workers in the café screamed and shouted simultaneously.

A separate airliner hit the other tower as a massive ball of fire rolled and erupted. People rolled in more televisions with all the networks covering this event. Many were calling for answers. They said on the news that the President was in Sarasota and was due to speak. What the hell is he going to say Jonas thought we are clearly under attack. The air base they were at went into immediate lockdown. Everyone was glued to the television in disbelief for hours about two more planes one hitting the pentagon and another crashing into the countryside of Pennsylvania.

Above the flames in both towers were people hanging out of the windows waving for help. It didn't take long for the real terror to begin. The network cameramen started filming people leaping out of the windows. Everyone watching in the cafeteria was a gasp at that sight. Another person made the hard decision and jumped from a window of a burning tower. Their torso fluttered in their death fall. Imagine what that person had to of felt before making the decision of what was a hard reality Jonas thought. A Hispanic woman crying came up to Jonas and few others.

"Oh my, oh my lord we have to pray for these people. We must pray for these people." she said.

He overheard two men talking.

"I bet it is so hot from that jet fuel inferno that the only thing to do is jump." "Damn it to hell, it is obscene to put this on television for kids to watch."

Just as he made that comment the first tower gave way, what seemed to be a massive crumble, it took what seemed ten seconds to crumble to the street level and then exhausting a huge dust cloud. The scene was something out of a movie with men and women running from the dust cloud until they disappeared in it. It seemed not twenty minutes later the other tower collapsed with the same effect. Later in life Jonas told his son that the terrorism that day would impact the world for the next fifty years.

The mayor of New York City was being escorted with a news crew and a live microphone since the ten o'clock hour. The man operated like a machine with people coming at him from all directions. People who worked for him with question upon question he immediately had the answer. He knew which operations center was up and running and who had what responsibility. Where the back up operations center was and who was in charge and where to go if they lost power. He knew the re-routes of public transportation and had already spoken live to the majority of the media regarding the current state emergency services. Alerting to everyone to try to keep calm in a situation that was anything but.

Jonas watched the agents run passed him back out to the hangar. He followed them to the office with the television. Salas was on the phone and Cabrera seemed to be hanging by a thread waiting for word. Jonas knocked and entered the office he only could hear what Salas was saying.

"Dan, Dan listen to me. Listen. I have a sniper down there now. The ransom and drop guy are with me. The seal team will be in position in approximately ten hours everyone has been briefed you can not…..what?"

"Who the hell told you that? Has that been confirmed?" Salas turned around and saw Jonas in the office and immediately motioned to Cabrera to have him leave the room. "Sorry doc." Jonas stepped out and walked outside to the runway. It had been loud early on with a lot of traffic and now dead quiet it was eerie. He turned back and Salas and Cabrera were standing there behind him. Salas had just closed his phone.

"Hey Doc got a second?" He walked over to them. Salas began to fidget with his tie and looked to the hangar floor.

"We, uh." He had to gather himself.

"Unfortunately our intel confirms the death of Ms. Adams." Jonas just stood with a blank face.

"No, no. Can't be it's me his wants, he wants me dead." He turned away. Tears ran down his cheeks. He became lightheaded for a moment.

"Doc we have someone undercover posing as a working girl who confirmed it early this morning. She also confirms that Rico then left the port-o."

Jonas erupted with anger he shouted at the agents. "You took too long analyzing the fucking video and now Jess is dead, and you two fucking bastards can explain all of this to her family!"

He paced back and forth and then bent his knees holding his face in disbelief. He didn't think Rico would actually kill her. Everyone is getting the news of a lot of death today, why not one more he thought.

"I'm sorry as hell doc," Cabrera said. Salas looked at Jonas. He finally looked at him again. "I am very sorry, very sorry for your loss."

"Yeah, you can save the sorry for Patty and Roger." He walked away from them up the side of the runway, the agents went back in hangar. He thought of the gorge of all things. Sirens from emergency vehicles sounded in the distance.

Chapter 26

Over half a decade had come and gone and he was fishing with his young son on the beach at the cabin. His mother Sara took pictures of them. She stood there on the back deck of the cabin with her pregnant daughter in-law.

"Oh, I meant to ask about your sister and her family. Jonas told me you have a traditional ski trip over the winter break."

"Yes. Michelle her husband Colin and they have a little girl Maureen. We go off to Vermont for half that week in February. The kids have fun. The parents drink."

The two laughed. "Oh look do they have a bite? Oh no, too bad." Sara looked to Ashley.

"Did you know that in the summer 79' Jim and Jonas reeled in a 20 pound catfish?"

"He briefly mentioned it." Ashley said smiling.

"Well I watched the whole thing, it was hot out just like today. I was scared to the death it took them over an hour from right down there at the beach. That year we had a lot of rain, the river was higher than normal with a lot of debris.

Jim kept getting snagged on tree limbs. He would hand the fishing pole off to Jonas and follow his line into the river, he did this two or three times. But they finally reeled the fish in."

She waved at them fishing.

"Jim was so proud of him. He told that story at every truck stop he hit for years to come and giving the credit to Jonas. He just seemed to know what to do with the rod, the reel, the drag. He kept calm and knew how to handle the pressure. Jonas was really something to watch."

"I bet he was." She looked to the beach.